The Darkness

In the Light

A Provocative Series by Tony Nalley
Based on a True Story

THE DARKNESS IN THE LIGHT

"Two young hearts are torn apart by the brutal actions of their Church's Youth Minister. One could not tell her secret, and the other could not know. Bound by a promise made to one another in a little church in Michigan, both of their lives are changed forever. When they are re-united years later …and their passions are rekindled, neither realizes just how distant their lives …and their very souls have become. Murder, mystery, romance, and witchcraft abound in this modern-day novel. It is a psychological drama with a paranormal twist."

T. N.

THE DARKNESS IN THE LIGHT

from the author

"The premise of this writing is to create emotion within the reader. Too many times do we as a society, encompass depth of meaning into single solitary words, rape, sodomy, molestation. It is easier as a society to set aside the emotional trauma and lifelong repercussions inside a distinct and legal term or analogy and dismiss it once the perpetrator has been sentenced."

"These acts of violence have far reaching ramifications that often change the psychological makeup of the victim; their lives, the lives of those around them …and their future lives. It alters the universal timeline and reality."

"It is much easier to say that the criminal needs to be put away than to understand the seriousness and complexity of their actions. Because, if you were to see what happened, if you were allowed to peer into the mind of both the perpetrator and the victim, the criminal would not get off so easy with mere jail time. Their entrails would be burned, their bodies would be hung, and they would be buried in unmarked graves."

"This series is a work of fiction, though many of the events are based upon factual occurrences. All names and locations have been changed to protect the innocent. And no emotional, spiritual, societal, or physical harm is intended or implied."

"These crimes never happened to me. But similar transgressions have happened to others around me."

"The consequences were devastating. They have affected my life, and they have touched and changed countless other lives."

"In many ways we are all connected. The air we breathe. The steps we take. The paths we choose are all intertwined."

"Like a single drop of rain upon the water, what happens to one of us has rippling effects upon us all."

Tony Nalley

National Suicide Prevention Lifeline
Call 1-800-273-8255
Available 24 hours a day

National Child Abuse Hotline is available 24/7 at (1-800) 4-A-Child or (1-800) 422-4453

National Sexual Assault Hotline
Call 1-800-656-4673
Available 24 hours a day

TONY NALLEY

♫ The world was on fire, and no one could save me but you. It's strange what desire will make foolish people do. I'd never dreamed that I'd meet somebody like you. And I'd never dreamed that I'd lose somebody like you. No, I don't want to fall in love. No, I don't want to fall in love with you. ♫

♫ What a wicked game you played to make me feel this way. What a wicked thing to do to let me dream of you. What a wicked thing to say you never felt this way. What a wicked thing to do to make me dream of you. And I don't want to fall in love. ♫ Wicked Game - Chris Isaak

THE DARKNESS IN THE LIGHT

...a foreshadowing

On a stone arch bridge in Bowman's Hill, he sat upon its balustrade. The rocks were cold. And the sounds of the waters from the river below reverberated, as they crashed against the stone and mortar, creating an atmosphere of mist and rushing winds. He dangled his legs over the side.

"I love you. You know I love you, right?" He said as he turned to her.

"Yes." She answered as a shadow filled her eyes.

"I don't know if I can do this." He said as his hands caressed the stones.

"You can." She encouraged.

"What happens on the other side?" He asked.

"Sanctuary," she answered.

He looked deeply into the eyes of the girl, who'd lain naked in his arms, only moments before. She made him feel vibrant and alive. She gave him power. She made him feel young and invincible. In return, she fed upon his freedom of will, drawing him in, bringing his mind and body to unimaginable levels of enlightenment and pleasure.

13

She exposed his soul. She revealed his secrets. She relieved his pain.

He penetrated her secret places; and filled her primal urges, forcing her to moan, and quiver uncontrollably.

With each primordial thrust he exploded with furor, deep within her velvet walls, filling her essence with his passion.

"I'll do this for you." He said as he looked down upon the river. "I love you."

She did not reply. She wondered how many scars she'd justified, because the one, who said he'd loved her, had wielded the knife.

"Promise me." He begged her.

She did not reply.

"Promise me." He shouted. "Babydoll, promise me." He pleaded.

Cold chills.

The resonating sound of the name.

Darkness filled her mind and spirit.

"I promise my honey." She replied and then paused, "Paradise."

14

He gazed into her eyes one final time; a final time, before he flung himself over the railings.

His love.

His gift.

Her sacrifice.

Below the gray stone bridge, her lover's body met the rolling waters, and his life's blood left him. She wiped away a tear slowly with her sleeve, and she breathed a heavy sigh as she peered out into the gloom.

And there came a glimmer of peace, a solitary moment of calm; though not one of remorse. It was a moment of liberation; a release so overwhelming that it caused her heart to remember.

She remembered who she had once been.

And she remembered when she could, feel.

Then, she turned slowly from where he had fallen upon the waters deep, and she moved quietly, disappearing like a ghost …vanishing into the darkness.

THE DARKNESS IN THE LIGHT

Chapter One – A Deeply-Seated Flame

The whole world seemed to have stopped as their eyes met across the crowded room. After all these years Tommy still loved her, and Tara knew instinctively, she could see it in his eyes. She could always see it in his eyes.

He excited her. She felt a rush ...a lifetime filled with emotions screaming through her veins again, and it scared her. It scared her to death.

His pulse quickened as he approached her. His heart pounded deep within his chest, as his face began to blush.

Her breathing increased; with every step he took closer to her. Time became fragmented, as a million thoughts entered her mind, but no words, she could think of no words. He reached for her hand, and she gave it to him willingly.

She was trembling with anticipation. She wanted to be there at that moment with him, though at the same time she also wanted to run. She wanted to run far, far away.

But how could she run? She was in a wheelchair. Where could she go? What could she do as the eager flashes of memory danced through her mind, like irrational moments of expectation?

She could do nothing but look up at him, look up into his caring and loving green eyes and try to form her words.

17

"Hello, Tommy." She whispered as he slowly leaned into her, pressed his lips against the softness of her skin and tenderly kissed her hand.

"I have missed you." He whispered in her ear as though he had been waiting for a lifetime to speak those words.

And he had been waiting. He had been waiting for this moment, for all his life. "I have missed you in my life," he whispered again.

"I have missed you too." She replied lovingly while reaching for him to come into her embrace.

They held one another in those few moments for what felt to them both like an eternity. As their lips touched, their souls embraced for a lifetime. Intuitively, they realized they had ignited a deeply seated flame within one another; a flame that had been kindled in their youth, building, and growing within their souls with a passion and intensity they could no longer contain.

They did not speak words. They did not have to.

When he first kissed her, he kissed her very, very softly, like she was a dessert and he wanted to savor every mouthful of her. Then, he lay her down …and within moments they were in one another's arms …in lovers embrace, out of sight, beneath the flickering shadows of a single candle's light.

Tommy kissed her again and she fell into him, this time with a lover's passion, desire and appetite.

Undressing each other hurriedly, with their kisses and their lips never parting, they came together with passionate and eager enthusiasm.

The rush of excitement between them was matched only by her squeals of delight and his want of pleasure. Their bodies connected intimately, he in her and her on him.

He kissed her ardently, holding her steadfastly in his arms, securely and lovingly within his embrace. He found her softness, her tightness, and his intensity increased with each piercing thrust.

In heated waves of fiery obsession, they reached climax together, and lay lovingly in one another's arms, still deeply and intimately connected, with warmth of frenzy filling their minds, and her beautiful body.

He had made her feel things she had no longer thought she could feel. She had been made love to, and she had felt his love and passion with his every touch.

With heartbeats pounding, exhausted from the fervor, they lay joined in a familiar union of body and soul.

And they breathed in the ecstasy of one another's scents, touches and tastes.

"I'm so glad you've come back into my life." Tara whispered softly through sultry breaths of passion.

"What do you remember of me?" Tommy asked. "What do you remember of us?"

She turned her eyes away from him as her fingers caressed his chest.

"Do you remember what happened?" He asked again as he lifted her chin for their eyes to meet.

"You …are …my …memory." She replied.

How do hearts become strangers after they've touched souls?

Throughout his whole life, Tommy had been unable to love as deeply as he had loved her.

His heart still belonged to her.

Because she had been the one who had broken it.

TONY NALLEY

THE DARKNESS IN THE LIGHT

Chapter Two – The Promise

"Coming back here …it's filled with ghosts." Tommy thought, as he turned his car down an old familiar road.

After last night's chance meeting with Tara, he felt a need to revisit some of their old haunts and stomping grounds.

He knew this location very well. He remembered the sights, the sounds, and the smells as though it were only yesterday. As it came into view, he parked his car along the edge of the road and walked through the tall grass to an old wooden fence, connected by a large black iron chain, which stood like a guardian overlooking the green fields.

The elementary school buildings were empty and foreboding, with a hint of shadows lurking just behind their walls, peeking out through their windows.

The school yard was empty as well, and it appeared abandoned. Its swings swayed back and forth with each small gust of wind that sent an eerie chill down his spine.

He envisioned children from its past, small ghosts running to and fro upon the playground, taunting one another in fun, laughing and playing.

He had first met her here. He remembered how much she loved to run. She had a free and spontaneous spirit, and he so adored her. He remembered her running past him,

23

teasing him, and challenging him to chase her. He fell in love with Tara here, though he was far too young at the time to understand what love was, or what his feelings for her truly meant.

"Love and life were so much simpler then." He said aloud, so he could feel his thoughts escape his mind.

He would not find it here, but somewhere within him, he knew he was searching for something he had missed; something that had eluded him. He longed for some sense of reason or some spark of memory that would yield a clairvoyant thought or at the very least, some form of a fairy-tale resolution. But there was none.

Behind him stood the junior high school building, it was solemn and unnatural looking in appearance. It stood three stories high and was made of mortar and solid concrete. Its architecture was reminiscent of a military prison, rather than that of a school built to educate children. It was painted a creamed color of white that stood in direct contrast, to the darkening blue backdrop of rain clouds that were forming and moving slowly across the sky. He could remember the sounds of the bells as they would ring and the roar of his classmates as they hurriedly clamored within its hallways. He imagined its emptiness, now that its doors were locked and tightly sealed; and of the echo that would resonate off its walls, if but a single coin were to be dropped upon its floors.

He had once carried Tara up its long and winding stone staircase. She had been in an accident. Her right leg had

24

been sprained in a fall while running and she had been using crutches to help get from class to class. But it was difficult for her to climb the stairs. He recalled her excitement when he offered to carry her, and how light she seemed as he cradled her in his arms to the second floor. He remembered the feeling of being her 'knight in shining armor', as she snuggled playfully against his neck. She made him feel strong and masculine. He would always remember that about her; how she made him feel.

And he would also remember how sweetly she smelled of lavender and honeysuckles.

As rain began to fall in cold droplets to the ground, Tommy returned to the comfort and shelter of his car and started the engine. There was another place he needed to see. He had not been there in a very long time either.

The windshield wipers made a screeching sound upon the glass with a repeated dragging rhythm of rubber, as he exited the school's parking lot and made his way through the drizzle. He remained deep in thought as he drove, remembering times long past.

The sounds of his tires on wet pavement filled his senses as did the smell of rainwater in the air, coming in through the crack of his window.

The graveled lot was empty as he pulled into a parking space and turned his headlights on high. The church sat dark upon the hill as his beams of light flickered and danced through the falling rain upon its brick walls. Its steeple reached upward to great heights in the sky; though it bore no cross, its structural design was outlined against the gale. This place was well-known to him, a familiar place, and it opened a floodgate of forgotten memories and feelings.

He remembered Tara the most when she was here. He remembered her laughter, her playfulness and their many wonderful conversations together. He also recalled her quick wit and epic sense of humor.

She made him laugh.

He made her laugh.

They had been kids together here.

Within this church, Tommy had been baptized into a new church family. And it was also here, beneath the lights of a Christmas tree, in December of his thirteenth year that he and Tara had kissed for the very first time.

He remembered the touch of her lips, as he kissed her. He remembered kissing her, as though it were only moments ago, and of how she excited him with her playfulness and sweet innocence. He remembered the touch of her lips, her taste, and the love he saw, in her beautiful brown eyes.

Tommy jumped with fright as the thunder clasped.

Lightening dashed brightly across the sky, revealing the outline of the large Maple tree they once had played beneath as children. He remembered how they had spent countless hours together there, talking and sharing one another's hopes and dreams beneath the shelter of its leaves.

Tara would often read him bible stories, and he would listen as they lay on a blanket beneath it, as he stared out into the cloudless sky.

Once he had found her sitting cross legged and barefoot on the floor of one of the Church's small rooms filled with children, little ones climbing here and there across her shoulders and back, and then up and onto her lap, as she would read to them, nursery rhymes, about Jesus and the miracles of the world. Tara was a gentle and loving soul. And he had been her best friend; her confidant. But for Tommy, Tara was his heart.

It was just after the church's Christmas pageant that year, a couple of months before her fourteenth birthday that he noticed a change in her. She began to distance herself from him, making apologies for not returning his calls, and she began changing the plans they had made without any excuse or an explanation.

He recalled how she began avoiding him. He knew she had become more deeply involved in her recently given church duties and responsibilities, but what he could not understand at the time was why she had simultaneously isolated herself from him.

She had distanced herself completely from him, both physically and emotionally, right after that pageant.

It hurt him deeply, but he gave her room to breathe.

With the car still running, Tommy turned on the heater and warmed his hands and fingers with its vent. The temperature had dropped dramatically after the storm had taken hold, though he had not paid close attention to the change. He lit up a cigarette and his windshield fogged up, so he rolled his window down a little to help it defrost. And he inhaled a long draw from his cigarette causing its fire to glow a bright red.

He wondered if she remembered what happened.

Though he did not think it would be possible for her to forget.

It was the summer; after they had first kissed, right before their freshman year in Junior High School. They had embarked on a week-long journey together. It was on their Church's youth mission trip, to help with a fledgling church's vacation bible school program. They spent a week together in another state with about forty other kids, but it had been Tommy's hope and intention while there, to find some time to be alone with her, at least for a moment, so he could talk with her and sort things through.

The sister church was a pleasant school-like building nestled into a residential neighborhood filled with many dark green drooping willow trees. It was raining when they arrived.

"Much as it's raining now." He thought to himself as he exhaled another breath of smoke.

Down the hallway of this little church building, he caught a glimpse of Tara, one afternoon, just as she turned the corner and disappeared into a little side room. It was a small room with large windows, that he believed the congregation had used for preschool classes during their Church's sermons on Sunday mornings. It was filled with all manner of Christian books and toys for children, with pictures scattered about haphazardly upon its walls. He knew the room well, because he had spent several nights trying to sleep on its hardwood floors.

The church was empty except for her and him. And he thought it could be the pivotal point and deciding moment; a perfect time to confess his undying love for her.

His legs trembled all the way down the hallway as he hurried to catch up with her,

She was facing away from him when he entered the room. She was barefoot and wearing a pair of tight purple shorts that hugged the curve of her hips very nicely.

She was gorgeous. She was fourteen years old, and he absolutely adored her. Her hair was brown and straight and fell just past her shoulders in length. Her legs were tanned a beautiful auburn. He loved her long legs and thought to himself that her skin appeared to have been kissed by the sun.

She stood with her back to him for a moment, facing toward the closed curtained windows ...and Tommy froze in his tracks.

Tara, the love of his life, was standing in the arms of another guy, a much older man, and he was kissing her. And she ...was kissing him.

He recalled this moment very vividly, feeling his heart breaking as he struggled to find reason. The man she was kissing was the church's Youth Minister. He met his gaze, but he said nothing. He looked at Tommy, with a smirk on his face, and simply walked out of the room.

"Please don't tell anyone, Tommy." Tara begged him as she turned to him, buttoning up her blouse and straightening up her shorts. "Promise me you won't tell." She didn't know if he had seen where her boyfriends' hands had been. "Dan will get into so much trouble if you tell."

She pleaded with her eyes; they begged him not to tell.

Tommy committed to memory how his body reacted to the immense conflict that raged within him. And he went numb with shock, as his mind tried to process what he had seen. He remembered looking deeply into her beautiful brown eyes, after what seemed an alarming amount of time had passed, and he promised her that he wouldn't tell.

"I promise," were the only words that would escape his throat.

It was in those fleeting moments that he rationalized, as a fourteen-year-old boy, what true love was all about. He reasoned that "Love was the strength and courage to put someone else's happiness over your own. It meant allowing that one person in the whole world that you loved, to be happy, even if it's not with you."

He never told a single soul after that.

He made himself forget.

And he buried this memory within his subconscious.

He had felt no guilt or remorse for keeping her secret at the time, although he now questioned the outcome had he not done so.

He was only fourteen years old; she had sworn him to secrecy, and he had given her his word. Although, upon re-evaluation from a grown-up point of view, he understood his mistake, and felt its pain.

Thunder roared, and flashes of lightening streaked across the night sky as Tommy drew his last drag of tobacco from his cigarette and flung the butt out the opening through his window into the rain.

He lost himself in his recently uncovered memories, as he drove away. And he turned the radio on for comfort, although the music did not give him any.

"What was the price of keeping my word?" He wondered.

Indeed, what had it cost him?

But more importantly …what had his promise cost her?

TONY NALLEY

THE DARKNESS IN THE LIGHT

Chapter Three – The Grooming of Tara

Dan was a good man. At least that's what he told himself.

He had some issues, he knew that, but it wasn't like he was worse than anybody else. He had become a Youth Minister and had graduated from the Southern Baptist Theological Seminary after college in Campbellsville.

He had traveled across the country, helping small churches build their youth memberships, to increase the overall size of their congregations. His position gave him the access and reputation he needed.

He believed in a god, and he knew he was forgiven for all of his sins.

Although he did not believe in a definitive good or evil, he did believe that if evil truly existed, it wouldn't arrive dressed as the devil. Besides, he believed Christians no longer lived as though Satan was real.

He was born without remorse or regret. He had no depth of feeling other than for his own. He wasn't a product of his environment. He was a created being. Therefore, he could be justified in his mind, in the blaming of the God of the bible, for his actions.

He could feel no shame and he accepted no responsibility for his behaviors.

His blatant disregard for what he termed as "God's morality," allowed him to focus on his own needs and gratifications. He didn't label himself as having a psychopathic personality, because that would be ridiculous.

He was a good man and he repeatedly told himself that.

Tara wasn't his first, but she was the youngest he had ever trained. He didn't call it grooming, because that sounded like brushing hair. He trained them up in the way they should go. It was biblical, and it was his first rule.

He had met her at a congregational gathering during Christmas break when she was thirteen years old.

He was new to the Church, and she was beautiful; however, you'd qualify a thirteen-year-old as beautiful.

She was four foot eight and a half inches in height, and she was ninety pounds soaking wet.

She was Babydoll pretty, slim, perky and she had a bubbly personality. She also had an adorable smile and long straight brown hair. And he wanted her.

He was introduced to her as the Church's new Youth Minister. Most kids related to him quickly, because he didn't speak to them or treat them like they were children. It didn't take him very long to become friends with Tara, and in no time at all she had begun to trust him.

He needed her to trust him. That was very important. It was one of his rules. She had to trust him.

He talked with her nearly every day after they had met; both about church issues and activities as well as about more personal things. But mostly he would listen to her.

Being the Youth Minister had its advantages. The kids' parents trusted him with their children without question and in return, their kids trusted him as a grown-up, an adult.

Dan was funny and easy to talk to and all the young girls found him to be quite handsome. But his eyes were focused on Tara. He was going to have her. She was special.

So, he treated her that way. He treated Tara very specially.

He made it a point for her to know how amazing he thought she was. He always made time for her. He always listened to her, her thoughts, her problems, her hopes and dreams. He spoke with her as though she were an adult. He shared some of his secrets with her and he kept the secrets she shared with him.

Tara's home life was stressful. Her mom had always been tough on her. She talked with Dan about things like that, and he made her feel as though he was listening.

She also talked to him about the love she felt for a boy named Tommy.

The boy was a threat to Dan's plans for Tara. He needed to sever the ties that bound her to him. This kid could undo his training and ultimately …his power and control over her.

While he acknowledged her feelings for her childhood playmate, he simultaneously drove a wedge between them.

"Girls mature faster than little-boys do," he told her. "You don't need a small child in your life, a baby, an infant. You need a real man, someone who is more mature. You don't need a kid to play games with." He continued. "You need someone who will listen to you, protect you and keep you safe."

Every time Tara would mention his name, Dan would demean the boy's importance, character, and stature in her life. He knew in his teachings that if you lied well enough, and lied long enough, eventually, your lies would become someone's truth.

Tara trusted him. And he used her trust to manipulate her feelings and belief systems. Once he had broken her ties

38

with the boy, he could channel her emotions towards himself, and use her feelings to address his desires.

Dan was a pedophile, a psychopath and a predator.

Though he would never acknowledge the possibilities or ramifications of that diagnosis or think of himself in that manner.

And Tara was, in all respects, his perfect prey. She was young and enthusiastic and needed someone in her life to love and pay attention to her. Dan was isolating her from her family and her friends. It was a necessary process that would draw her closer to him and place him in control. It was another one of his rules.

Dan catered to Tara's every whim. He catered to her likes and her dislikes, bringing her chocolates and candies, and driving her to the movies, where they could spend time together. He was a man with specific needs and behaviors. And they needed to be fulfilled.

"Can you tell me something about you that you like about yourself." Dan asked her one evening while he drove her home from Church services in his car.

"I don't know." Tara replied. "I've never really thought about it. I guess I have a pretty smile and I'm really good with little kids and animals."

"You do have a pretty smile." He stated in response. "And you are very good with little kids and animals."

He looked to see Tara smiling at his words.

"So, what do girls your age look for in a guy?" Dan asked to get the conversation moving toward his purpose.

"We look for the same things all girls look for I guess," Tara answered. "It's who they are on the inside that matters the most, at least to me." She said as she placed her open hand to her heart. "Honesty is also very important." She continued. "And it's how good they treat you that matters the most. But it doesn't have to do with age." She interjected to let Dan know that she wasn't counting him off limits. "Some girls my age like older guys too."

"What about you, Tara?" He asked. "Do you like older guys?"

"Well, there is this one guy." She said bashfully. "He's really nice to me."

"Tell me about him. Do I know him?" He asked. "Should I be jealous?"

"You most certainly do not." Tara said with a cute playful laugh as she lightheartedly slapped him on his leg. "You do know him. He's tall and handsome, and I think I like him a lot."

Tara was twisting the ends of her hair nervously with her fingers, as she looked at Dan teasingly in the driver's seat. He looked very handsome to her. He made her

40

heartbeat fast and he caused her face to blush just thinking about him. She knew he was older than she was, and that he couldn't possibly like a young girl like her, but she didn't care about that. He made her feel special, and she liked him very much because of it.

He pulled the car through a drive-up window and ordered two large strawberry shakes. And then he drove into an adjacent parking place and shut off the car.

"I think I like someone too." He said as he looked at her. "She's younger than me, but I like her, and I care about her very much."

Tara was crushed. If he were in love with someone else, she would be devastated. She felt heartbroken.

"What will I do?" She thought. "Who can I turn to?"

"What do you think we should do about it?" Dan asked her as he looked into her eyes.

For the first time, Tara realized that he was speaking about her. She became instantly excited and bounced around on the passenger seat, so she could face him directly, and she sat cross legged on his faux leather seats.

"I think we should take it slow." Tara said quickly, and then she spoke calmly and slowly to make herself sound more grown-up and convincing. "And just see how it goes."

41

"But no-one can know, Tara." Dan stated. "If anyone finds out, I'll lose my position and possibly go to jail. You're a beautiful and amazing girl, but you're also underage. It would kill my career."

"Then we won't tell anyone." Tara reasoned. She moved closer to him as she spoke, kneeling on the seats with her face close to his, daring him to kiss her. "We'll keep it a secret. I'm great at keeping secrets." She said suggestively.

It was the first time they kissed. And it was her idea. Dan wanted it that way. It was one of his rules.

Over the next few months, Tara was in total and complete Heaven. She had an older boyfriend who listened to her, took her places, protected her and made her feel like she was safe and wanted.

He made her feel warm, older and loved.

Dan was taking his time, getting her ready. It was a necessary process for him to train her correctly. It was one of his rules. But it was getting harder for him to hold back.

He had to keep himself in control.

That's what it was all about. It wasn't about his desire to be with Tara. It was primarily about his desire to have power and control over her. He needed it. He needed to have total and complete …power and control.

Tara's first time had to be special. She would need a memory to be so overwhelming and wonderful that it would curl her toes, each time she thought about it. It would need to be a moment so incredible that no matter the wrongs he did to her afterward, he would be forgiven, and everything would be made right between them.

Dan was devising a plan, creating an opportunity to have Tara all to himself, overnight, for just such an experience.

He told a little white lie to his Church Pastor, nothing too elaborate or detailed as to cause alarm if he were to be questioned. It was a simple lie, about teaching a bible study class for a youth group the following weekend.

The lie took him off his Church's calendar and it provided cover if Tara's parents should happen to call.

They never called. Her parents were thrilled to have their daughter doing something she loved to do. And they believed it was good for her, to acknowledge God's will and help with a sister Church.

"Amen." Dan said to himself with a chuckle. "If they only knew."

Dan was an Autumn, and she was a Spring, and she knew older guys needed physical love and affection from their women.

She was his woman. He had told her this, many times.

43

An hour outside of Fredericksburg, Dan pulled his car into the parking lot of an extremely nice and very expensive Lake Resort Inn. It was highlighted by grand trees and regal architecture. It was decorated in lights that twinkled like diamonds and shimmered upon the waters of its lake. By its entrance, a huge fountain gushed water and mist into the nights sky. Tara's eyes widened as she walked through its doors, and she marveled at its huge, majestic columns and marbled floors.

As they reached the lobby, Dan spoke with the pretty hostess dressed in proper attire about the room he had reserved.

"We'd like to check in, please." Dan said politely. "We have a reservation under the last name of Patterson."

"Yes Sir." The hostess replied as she checked her registrations. "We have a reservation for you and your lovely daughter in our Royal suite, room three-fifteen."

Tara giggled. She never thought her boyfriend could be mistaken for her father. She realized he was older, but he was only twenty-seven. She could tell he liked the sound of it though, because it caused him to get an erection. She noticed.

"Thank you." Dan replied as he accepted the key and received directions to the room.

As Dan turned from the Hostess Station, Tara ran teasingly across the hotel's lobby to the elevators, and playfully yelled, "I beat ya." And then she pushed the white arrow button as she stood and waited for him to catch up.

When the doors opened they stepped inside and looked at one another mischievously. Tara jumped up into his arms and wrapped her legs around his waist and kissed him as the elevator doors closed shut.

The room was nice. It had a large king-sized bed in the center and a full-sized Jacuzzi bathtub and stand-up shower in the bathroom. The mahogany entertainment center held a fifty-inch television screen. And Dan had ordered flowers to be strategically placed throughout.

The air was filled with the aroma of softly scented candles.

Tara felt like a princess.

"What do you think?" Dan asked as he looked at his beautiful young prize.

Tara kicked off her shoes and climbed up into the middle of the bed and said, "I love it." Then she threw her arms up as she fell backwards upon the pillows and landed with a bounce.

Her youthfulness and playfulness excited him almost as much as her innocence.

Going forward, she would do as she was told. She was his to command. He was in control. And no matter what happened, she would believe it was her fault, because it had been her choice. She had been made to believe that she was making the decisions.

And that was all he truly needed.

He had rules that he needed to follow. He could not neglect or change them.

He was in complete control now.

Dan was a good man. At least that's what he told himself.

TONY NALLEY

Chapter Four – The Wooden Cross

Beside a hand carved wooden cross near the swing on her back porch, Tara sat in her wheelchair, and looked out over the green fields and hills of grass.

A small black heifer and her newborn calf stood under a small shade tree near the top, as her two large dogs sat on this side of a fence that enclosed them, with eyes and ears focused on their every move. She knew at any moment, one of them would take off chasing after the mama and her calf, and she would have to clap her hands loudly together and order them to stay in the yard.

Tara had made a comfortable life for herself. She lived in an upper middle-class home with her two beautiful daughters, Heather, and Hope. Her girls were smart and funny and were born with her beauty, and their father's eyes.

It was here upon these rolling fields that she and Michael, her soon to be ex-husband, lived, and had raised their children over the past fourteen years.

The large brick contemporary house was nestled in an open country field; back a long-graveled driveway. It sat peacefully between the thick timbers of Crawly Hill near the winding waters of Miller's Creek; a stone's throw from a mystical tree known as the Old Jenny Tree.

The Old Jenny Tree is an ancient wood that has the resemblance of a Donkey's face, with ears that reach up

49

and out as large branches to Heaven. Jenny is the name of a female donkey. She had dark eyes and a long equine nose. Legends said that it was haunted and if you touched it, you would die. Other stories claimed that if you looked into the eyes of the Old Jenny, you would become possessed by the evil spirits that lay within her. Some knew it as the Old Donkey Tree.

Tara absolutely loved this tree. She loved anything that involved ghosts and spirits and the supernatural.

The air was fresh this morning, as she sipped her coffee, and the skies were painted a beautiful blue after last night's storms. The puffy white clouds were motionless, though the winds were cool and brisk as they blew against her skin.

She hadn't heard from Tommy since they had made love two nights ago.

But she couldn't seem to get him out of her mind.

He had become even more handsome than she had remembered. He had a touch of gray in his hair, naturally, but that only made him appear more distinguished and attractive. It was his eyes though, his haunting green eyes, more than anything else that brought back the boy in him, she had once known.

"You are the air that I breathe." He had said to her. The boy was still there, hiding inside the man that he'd now become.

Tommy was her one true love, although she would never allow herself to admit it. Her feelings were strong for him, and they had been from the moment he had chased her around the playground when they were kids, but she wouldn't call it love.

Love for her was only a term of endearment, a word for affection and deep down she never truly believed in words. Words too often became lies. Though truthfully, she never felt she was good enough for him. So, she had pushed him away, even when she wanted to pull him close.

She kept him at a distance because she didn't want to hurt him. And she didn't want him to learn who she had become, what she had done, because he would never look at her the same; the way he had looked at her the other night, the loving way he had looked at her all her life.

He asked her if she remembered what happened between them. She knew he would bring it up, but she wasn't prepared to answer at the time. But of course, she remembered. She had relived those moments countless times throughout her lifetime. But she had never spoken of them to anyone.

It was one of her rules.

They say it's not what people think of you or what happens to you that determines who you will become. But that it's what you allow that defines you. Tara had been defined, consumed, and imprisoned all her life by what she had allowed.

The moment Tommy had found her in the arms of the Church's Youth Minister on the Mission trip when she was fourteen years old, was one of the most humiliating moments of her life. She was so embarrassed. She didn't know how long he had been standing there or what he might have seen. She could not speak with him about it. She was so traumatized.

The man had groomed her, as she would later understand the term, for months before anything had ever happened between them.

Being a man of the church, Dan was well educated and well versed in the arts of communication and persuasion.

His position had given him access to her schedule, her parents, her friends, and her life. As the Youth Minister he had even been allowed to stay overnight at her home while her parents were away.

Dan was an upstanding member of the community, and everybody respected him. He was revered by her family, her friends, and her Church.

Tara loved the attention he gave her. He made her feel older and secretly sexy. Their relationship began and happened in plain sight of everyone, as did the escalating abuse.

After Tommy had been sworn to secrecy and had left the children's nursery room in the Church in Michigan, Tara waited. She knew that Dan would be returning soon and that he would be angry. She hadn't understood him lately. He had changed over the past few months.

Once he had been the perfect boyfriend. He had been the one she could turn to for anything, he was her confidant.

She went to him for advice, for his protection and for his companionship. Just to have someone to listen to her, who was his age, was amazing to her. He was twenty-seven.

Dan had catered to her every whim. He had escorted her to Basketball games and Football games, and he had even taken her to see R-rated movies. He had bought her a pretty necklace with a heart on it. He was always buying her things. He was so nice. He had even given her gifts of an ankle bracelet and a toe ring to make her feel sexy.

And for her birthday he had bought her a real pair of diamond earrings.

Dan called her "Babydoll," when they were alone together, and it made her feel so warm and loved and special. He would bring her flowers and leave her little notes when she least expected it, to remind her that he was thinking of her and to show her how much he cared.

He was so good to her. And he told her that he loved her often.

Their relationship had remained a secret between them for almost eight months before Tommy had seen them together, because she was so much younger than he was.

They had become intimate, after her fourteenth birthday, as winter became spring.

Her parents would have killed her if they knew. It might have physically killed her dad if he had found out what she had been doing. And Dan would most definitely have lost his position, his career and possibly his freedom, if anyone had found out.

In Tara's mind it was all her fault. She was the one who had made the first move on Dan. It wasn't the other way around. She had been the one to kiss him first.

She loved him with all her heart, but everything was falling apart, and she didn't know how to fix it.

"Maybe," she had thought. "If I am more patient and more understanding things will go back to the way they had been."

She didn't understand the changes in him. Surely this was her fault too. She must have done something wrong.

She just didn't know what it was. He had become so distant and so demanding of her that it seemed no matter how hard she tried to please him, no matter what she said or did could make him happy again.

The door closed and locked behind her, just as she pulled the curtains open so the light from the summer sun could fill the room. Tara could see the others outside, including Tommy, as he waited in line at the barbeque table to fill his plate.

Dan came up from behind her, grabbing her by the waist and he whispered into her ear.

"You know I love you Babydoll, right?" He said as his hands began to wander.

"I love you too." Tara replied knowing where his actions would lead.

"You know I need this?" Dan whispered further.

Tara didn't say anything. She had become used to his advances

Between reason and madness, Tara thought she had gazed out through the open window for a moment and had met with Tommy's green eyes.

Tara returned from her thoughts of the past and sipped her final taste of coffee. Then she reached into her jacket pocket and took out her phone.

She checked her messages and texts, but there wasn't anything from him.

She realized it had only been a couple of days, but she really needed to hear his voice.

For the first time in forever, her body had been brought to orgasm in sweet ecstasy through the act of a man's tenderness and affection, rather than through his violence and abuse.

She wanted Tommy to know how he made her feel. She wanted him to know that he had made her feel alive. She had almost forgotten what it was like to feel alive; what it was like to be touched by someone who loved her. But she knew she would have to open up to him and explain her past; give him intimate details of her life.

"It's been a giant cluster-fuck." Tara said out loud. "What would he think of me then?" She thought to herself.

She chuckled at the thought of saying the words 'cluster-fuck' to Tommy, and she wondered if he remembered from their youth, how imaginative and colorful her vocabulary was. She always had a dark sense of humor, and a provocative way with words.

"It's part of my charm." She whispered to herself and smiled.

She closed her phone and called her dogs to come to her on the porch.

"Come here boys. Come on." She said clapping her hands together. "Come on, now."

"I'll text him if I haven't heard anything by nightfall." She thought to herself as her dogs came running.

She rubbed and petted them as they licked her arms and face and hands with excitement. Her animals loved her. They would always love her.

"In the meantime," she decided as she reached down for her empty mug. "I need something a whole lot stronger than Folgers in my cup."

Tara chuckled at her use of the familiar commercial jingle, and of her common use of the vernacular.

THE DARKNESS IN THE LIGHT

Chapter Five – Shattered Promises

As he opened the lofty glass doors, the bells jingled, and Tommy entered the Pancake Café just outside of Barstow.

It was six-thirty in the morning.

There was an old man sitting on a bar stool holding the day's paper, speaking with a much younger black woman, and a really cute waitress behind the counter.

They acknowledged one another as he walked in and closed the door.

Tommy looked around the small and dimly lit dining room and headed towards the seats by the windows. He had been driving for the last several hours. But he had only realized a few minutes before turning in, that he had become both cold and profoundly hungry.

The temperature inside the Café warmed him almost immediately. And the smell of the bacon and eggs on the grill was pleasing to his senses.

"I'll be right with you." The waitress said as she wiped off the counter and dried her hands with her apron. He motioned to her across the Café in the direction he'd be sitting.

The décor within the restaurant resembled that of a nineteen fifties style Diner, with cold steel tables and bright red vinyl seats. It had the feel of an older and different generation. Tommy found a corner booth and sat down and made himself comfortable. And he stared out through one of the room's tall plate-glass windows.

"What can I bring you this morning?" The young girl asked him moments later, as she stood patiently near his table. She was smiling with pen and paper in her hand, "Coffee?"

"Yes, a cup of coffee, please," He answered, "Black. And I'll have the breakfast platter with two eggs medium over easy, with bacon and toast."

"Will that be all?" She asked him, "Biscuits and gravy on the side?"

She noticed how attractive he was. She also noticed how well he filled out his ripped jeans the moment he had walked through the door.

"No, thank you. That'll be all." He said as he gave her a wink.

He turned again to watch the sun rising over the trees through the window; it brought with it a plethora of pastel colors in pinks and blues across the sky. And as the light of the dawn became rays of daylight, it cast reflections that sparkled and danced like millions of tiny beads of rain upon the grass. Last night's storm seemed to have washed the entire world clean.

"I never understood the story of Rip Van Winkle until now." He thought to himself. "I always thought it was about an old man who went to sleep for a hundred years and woke up to find his great-grand children playing beside him under a tree. I didn't realize that his eyes had been open for his whole entire life, but he had never truly seen. He was blinded by the life he was living and had not awakened to the blessings his life had to offer. And when he did finally open his eyes, metaphorically, it was too late. Everyone he loved was gone."

Over the past few nights, Tommy had been dealing with emotions and feelings he had long since forgotten. Seeing Tara again had re-awakened something inside of him, a longing he couldn't control. He hadn't slept. All night he had tossed and turned and wrestled with his demons. He hadn't been able to clear his brain of the thoughts, which had been running rampant through his mind.

The sounds and smells were invigorating as the waitress poured hot coffee into his cup. She noticed how masculine he smelled as she placed his breakfast plate on his table with a clatter.

Tommy thanked her again. She was pretty. She had a sparkle in her eyes that he had noticed right away. He said something funny, and she touched his arm as she laughed.

Her name was Allison.

He decided he would have cream and sugar with his coffee after all. So, he stirred them both in slowly, hearing the metal spoon clink against the sides of his smooth China cup. And he talked with her for a while.

"I don't know what it is yet, but there's something I like about you." He said as Allison sat down in the seat across from him twisting her hair.

"Oh yeah?" She said with a flirtatious grin. "What's not to like?"

Tommy knew he was pushing the line with his interactions, but she seemed to be playing along.

"See, right there," he answered suggestively. "If you keep talking like that I'm going to have to spank you."

"Maybe I might like it." She answered as her heart began to race.

"What am I going to do with you?" Tommy said smiling.

He quickly nodded towards the customers waiting by the counter to place their orders and to pay. Allison got up hurriedly to greet them. But as she walked, she turned to make sure he was looking.

He watched her walk. She had a nice ass.

The heat from the cup warmed his hands as he lifted it to his lips and took a sip. He didn't drink coffee very often,

62

but he felt a need this morning to feel its warmth and taste its soothing flavor.

"I can forgive myself for being young and naïve." He thought. "I can forgive myself for believing that keeping my word was as important as keeping a sacred oath. But I will never be able to forgive myself if my inaction caused her pain."

One of the hardest things Tommy had ever done was letting Tara go.

"I will call her today." He thought to himself.

He picked up his phone and thumbed through his contact list. Her number was there. Just as it had been an hour ago, and every hour since she had given it to him.

He opened his text messenger and looked for her name. It was there as well, just as it was before.

He wondered what he could say to her, "Hi. How are you?" It just didn't seem warm enough, and "hey, let's get married and have some babies", was entirely inappropriate.

The world had changed rapidly over these past few years.

No one talked to one another anymore. In an age when the entire world could communicate at the touch of a button, no one used their phone as a phone and spoke words. They would text one another. Often losing the meanings of what someone else has written because of spelling errors, the lack of punctuation or the hidden meaning of sarcasm behind the words. Tommy had a black belt in sarcasm and used body language when he said something funny.

Neither of these traits went over well using text.

After finishing his meal, Tommy wiped the corners of his mouth with his napkin and drank the last sip of coffee from his cup. He pulled a folded twenty-dollar bill from his front blue-jean pocket and laid it on the table to cover his tab. He nodded to Allison, who had signed her name and number on the back of his check with little hearts, and he placed it in his left shirt pocket. And he patted his pocket as he walked over to her.

"That looks amazing on you." He said to her as he motioned to her necklace. "And thanks for the number."

Allison bit her lip flirtatiously, as she played with her jewelry. She was cute. He wished he had listened to her more when they were talking. She had a nice smile.

"Call me." She mouthed with her lips. Tommy winked.

"I'd fuck her." He thought as he stepped outside and lit up a cigarette with his lighter; thankfully, she had given him her number.

"Nasty habit," he said in disgust with his next breath as he met the fresh air and inhaled deeply. "I should never have picked them back up." And then he sucked in another long drag and exhaled a huge puff of smoke.

As Tommy inhaled the tobacco and blew smoky rings into the morning, he suddenly remembered something.

He remembered words Tara had once spoken to him so many years ago.

"How could I have forgotten that?" He said aloud.

"Fuck you." She had said to him. "Fuck you." These were her exact words.

The memories now flooded his psyche. He wondered what else he may have forgotten.

"Why would Tara have said that to me? And why am I only now remembering this?" Tommy questioned himself as he wondered further.

His memories returned to him slowly, in little bits and pieces, small snippets like missing puzzle pieces of a much larger picture.

Tommy lit up another cigarette and leaned against the restaurant's wall.

He remembered teasing her playfully one afternoon as they sat in social-studies class. Tara was naturally flirtatious, and she playfully teased him in return. He tickled her to make her laugh. He loved the sound of her

65

laughter. He loved it when she was happy. He hadn't seen her happy in a long time. And he hadn't kissed her since Christmas.

"I've missed you Tara." He whispered to her as he rubbed and massaged her back. She was soft and always smelled of honeysuckles.

"So many things have happened, Tommy." She said to him. "I miss you too, I really do. But I don't know what I'm doing anymore."

"I love you." He whispered in her ear as he stroked her hair. "You don't have to say it back. I just need you to know how I feel. I love and adore you. I miss us. I miss you and me."

Moving gracefully to his words and the pleasure she was receiving, Tara lost herself in the ecstasy of Tommy's tender touch and his charms. Her body cherished the tingling sensations he was giving her, as the feel of his fingers ran electrically through her hair.

"Dan's too old for you." Tommy blurted out. "And I'm concerned about the promise I made." He said at last.

Tara heard what he said, but she processed his intentions differently. Her world had been in turmoil for a very long time. She loved Dan, but in many ways, she also feared him. She had no support at home. Her church family had been isolated from her and now, the only person she still felt she could trust was telling her that he was going to reveal her horrible secret.

Everyone, including her parents, would know how dirty she was. If they knew, she would be branded a whore, a slut. She already felt worthless enough as it was.

"Why would he do this to me?" She asked herself.

She couldn't allow it to happen. She wouldn't allow him to do this to her.

Tara jumped out of her chair and shouted at him in front of everyone in the classroom.

"Fuck you, Tommy." She shouted. "Fuck you."

She left him as quickly as the class bell sounded, without giving him a chance to respond. His classmates stared at him as they rose from their desks and exited the room.

And he and Tara never spoke of it again. But as his thoughts became feelings, he remembered the gut-wrenching pain that sunk deeply into his heart, the moment her words entered his spirit.

Words cut deep when you're young, especially when they come from someone you love.

Tommy dropped his cigarette on the pavement and put its fire out with the toe of his boot. As he walked to his car, he noticed how brightly the sun was shining, and how high it had risen in the sky, so he checked his watch for the time. It was almost nine-forty-five a.m. He had been there longer than he had realized.

He checked his contact list again for her number. It was still there.

He typed three words into a text message to her …and then he paused.

He put his sunglasses on and checked his look in his rear-view mirror, as he got in and shut his car door and turned on the car stereo. And a familiar song began to play.

♫ Hey, where did we go? Days when the rains came. Down in the hollow. Playing a new game. Laughing and a-running, hey, hey. Skipping and a-jumping. In the misty morning fog with our, our hearts a-thumping. And you, my brown-eyed girl. You, my brown-eyed girl. ♫

♫ Whatever happened to Tuesday and so slow? Going down to the old mine with a transistor radio. Standing in the sunlight laughing. Hide behind a rainbow's wall. Slipping and a-sliding. All along the waterfall with you, my brown-eyed girl. You, my brown-eyed girl. ♫
Sawyer Brown

As he listened he looked again at his phone, and before he could change his mind …he clicked send.

TONY NALLEY

THE DARKNESS IN THE LIGHT

Chapter Six – Child of Glass

In the junior high parking lot, the afternoon that Tara had screamed out at Tommy, Dan waited for Tara to get out of school. He waited for the bell to ring. He watched her walk out the small side doors to the left and head towards her bus. She was physically shaken when he blew his horn.

Dan wasn't good at reading people's feelings. He didn't have the ability.

He had no way of knowing that she had stormed out of her classroom, after shouting obscenities at Tommy, and had spent the last two periods crying her eyes out, in the girls' basketball, gym locker-room.

He had only been told that she had let the boy touch her.

Tara hadn't expected Dan to be there. But she opened his car door and sat down in the passenger seat beside him nonetheless; because there was something she wanted to tell him.

Dan was impulsive at times and Tara knew she had to adjust. After all, he was an older guy, and he was dating a younger girl. That alone would make him seem spontaneous, reckless and extremely unpredictable. He made her feel special in many ways.

Dating a guy who could drive was huge for a ninth-grade girl. Being with him made her feel older; though, it often made her feel out of control at the same time.

"I hear a boy has been touching you, rubbing your back during social-studies class." Dan said with a disgusted tone in his voice as her car door closed shut.

Tara was caught off guard by his comment, wondering how he had known.

"Does he have someone spying on me?" She thought.

"So, what else have you been doing with him?" He said condescendingly.

"Nothing," Tara stated in defense of his accusation, her eyes widening; her mind wondering where this conversation might lead.

Dan had changed since they had first met and kindled their relationship. And over the last six months he had become extremely mean to her, even violent at times. She thought about breaking it off with him, but he told her that he would tell her parents everything.

She couldn't let that happen. It would kill her dad. She still loved Dan, and she was trying very hard to work things out, but he was making her life miserable.

The car remained eerily quiet as Dan drove her through town. Music blared through the stereo speakers as she rolled down her window, to feel the rush of air blow through her hair. Soon he pulled the car down a tree covered back road on the way to her house. She recognized the road. She knew the place. They had been there before.

Tara dared not speak again. She could tell he was angry.

He had been angry with her often. She knew what he could do.

The car pulled to a stop in a far too familiar and secluded spot, which could not be seen from the main road. The path was not traveled or known by many.

"Get out." He demanded. Tara unlocked the door, and got out of the car, and she stood just outside the passenger door window.

Dan exited the vehicle, abruptly slamming his driver's side door with a bang. And then he walked around the front of the car with vigor to where she was standing.

As he walked towards her, her innermost spirit began to tremble uncontrollably. As he stood behind her, running his fingers through her beautiful brown hair and playing with the ends of it, she could feel the warmth of his breath through her hair, on the back of her neck.

"I thought I told you that you were mine?" He said to her in a whisper.

"Dan, please don't do this." Tara begged as tears began to roll down her cheeks.

She heard a knife click open and felt its cold steel blade.

"What are you doing?" Tara called out.

At first, Tara felt as though she were floating outside of her body, looking down upon herself.

"This wasn't happening." She thought. "How could this be happening? Oh my God. Please stop. Someone, please make him stop."

"Dan, please stop. Please." She cried.

Tara imagined herself in a different place, but all roads seemed to lead to this. She was lost and so completely alone.

"This is not me." She thought to herself. "This is not happening to me."

Her pain was immense.

And then, her body went limp. To all outward appearances, she was lifeless.

As Tara returned to her body and lay upon his cold black faux leather seats mostly naked, cold and abused with both of her eyes wide open, until the sun had set, and she was stimulated by the coolness of the night air.

It was then that her dreams became nightmares, and her visions became voices, as she lay in the backseat. Images of what had happened rushed back into her mind.

This wasn't the first time that Tara had been beaten. It also wasn't the first or last time that she would be raped.

She felt so alone, so ashamed, so dirty and yet so completely responsible for what she was allowing to happen. She felt within the depths of her heart, that she was completely and totally worthless.

Dan would take her home now and she would be expected to act as though nothing out of the ordinary had happened. He would tell her parents about how great she was and then he would talk about the church, say something amusing to make them laugh and then he would leave. And Tara would be left alone with the smell of him on her, sitting at the family dinner table, pretending that everything was all right and looking into the depths of her father's eyes, hoping upon all hopes that he didn't know.

"But how could he not know? He is my father. How can my mom and dad not smell Dan on me?" She thought.

The fact that Tommy knew what was going on made everything worse. He loved her, and she had cursed at him because of it.

"How can I face him?" She thought.

If there were a time in Tara's life that she could point to and say that this was the moment when she stopped believing in God, it was at this time. She stopped believing in herself and she stopped believing in God.

She was angry with him, and she questioned how a God would allow this to happen.

"What have I done to be treated with such hatred and malice?" She shouted in her mind.

She thought about killing herself. At least in dying she would be rid of him.

Within her psyche, her subconscious spirit, there came a rising darkness that swelled up within her. It caused her to laugh maniacally, as her mind cracked and shattered like many pieces of broken glass upon the floor. She envisioned herself as a porcelain doll, beautiful and fragile and so easily broken. But deep behind the doll's ceramic eyes she changed the vision.

In her darkened state, Tara created a new persona; a new and better child of glass, a "Babydoll", who would protect her heart and the innocence of her youth. She mentally accepted the darkness, of her own free will.

She would become different than she had been. She would become someone stronger and in control. She would use her sexuality as a tool, to further her wants and desires. And she would use her body and her promiscuity to manipulate, control and devastate any who would hurt her.

Tara would perfect the art of deception and become her father's perfect daughter, her school's perfect student and her lovers' perfect boy-toy.

Her thoughts ran fluidly as the darkness consumed her spirit.

She followed the car's headlights with her eyes, as they shined brightly and mixed with shadows upon her home, just as Dan pulled his car into her driveway. She didn't remember getting out of his car, but she loosely remembered an overwhelming feeling of power that came over her as if she were floating.

She closed her eyes that night after dinner and lay herself down on her bed; completely exhausted. She no longer prayed to God, so she prayed to the Angels before she fell asleep.

She prayed about a secret she had kept hidden in her heart.

And she thanked them for the courage they had given her, to keep her silence …about the baby.

THE DARKNESS IN THE LIGHT

Chapter Seven – Winged Angel

Beneath the shade of a large oak tree in her front yard, Tara sat in her wheelchair beside a winged Angel made of stone. The scene was sacred to her. She sought spiritual harmony below the branches of this tree. As the winds danced through the limbs above her, she could feel the coolness of the breeze as it revitalized her spirit.

She often came here early in the mornings for peace and solitude, and to visit the graves of her most treasured pets; her animals who now lay buried beneath the soil.

They had been part of her family. She loved them, and she missed them very much.

She found it difficult crossing the grass to this spot after dew had fallen or when she had been unable to mow, because the way was not smooth, and her driveway wasn't paved. But she would not complain. And she didn't. The accident, which had left her almost completely paralyzed from her waist down, had made her life a challenge, but it had not beaten her. She would not be defeated. If anything, the incident had forced her to become more assertive and active than most people who had the use of their legs, and full capability to walk. The obstacles she faced kept her mind lively and her body strong.

The car crash happened when she was fifteen years old. It was a very traumatic event in her life, it had changed everything, but it had not been the worst thing that had ever happened to her.

"This wheelchair is nothing," she often reminded herself as she envisioned her darkness.

Much greater things had been taken from her than her abilities to stand, walk or run.

She had named her adversary. It was one of her rules. She believed once you had given a name to it, you could defeat it. Her enemy, she called the 'darkness'.

Suddenly, Tara's iPhone pulsated and resounded with a ding. She reached for it on her lap, accidentally fumbling it with her hands and dropping it to the ground.

"Damn it." She exclaimed. "If I'd wanted it on the ground I would've put it there in the first place."

Holding herself steady in her chair, she leaned over its side and picked up her phone with the tips of her fingers and wiped it off with the soft cloth of her blouse. Her two large dogs' ears stood up at the sound of her voice and had instantly come running across the lawn to her side.

They sat at her feet and vied for her attention, as she checked her messages and read the sender's name under her breath.

The message was from Tommy.

"Good morning beautiful," were the much-welcomed words that brought a smile to her heart, as did the tickling sensations given to her by her dogs, as they licked her legs and her feet.

"Stop it." She commanded. "Stop. Stop." She said again as she pointed at them with her finger. They were both great dogs. But they were also very jealous of one another.

Susie was the youngest and she was the most active.

While Bear preferred to lie around and have the world come to him. Their licks were slobbery and wet, but even still, they were both very good and loving dogs.

Tara gave herself a few minutes to read and re-read Tommy's words. She wanted to answer him right away, but she didn't want it to appear as though she had been eagerly awaiting his message. Relationships were exceedingly difficult for her to maintain and understand.

Every one of them was different in their own strange and unique way, and her relationship with Tommy had been the most trying on her soul. She had pushed him away for most of her life because she truly didn't want to hurt him.

He had been the one she had cared about the most. And he would be the one she would hurt the most.

Susie and Bear stood at attention and barked noisily, as the sound of crunching rocks behind her caused her to turn to see whose car was pulling in her driveway. It was a wine-colored Volvo, her husband's car. She had almost forgotten about him. He traveled a lot on business.

Often, he was gone for weeks at a time. It didn't matter, they weren't close anymore. They hadn't been since their girls were little. He was their provider, and she gave him credit for that. He was also incredibly intelligent and made an enormous amount of money for the work that he did. But at home he was a stranger who lived upstairs, a closet alcoholic with a violent temper that she and her children feared.

She raised her hand and waved as he passed her by. Then she watched her dogs run after him, as he drove slowly up the driveway, to their two-car garage, and parked on the grass outside. He had been drinking. She could tell from the distance.

Michael staggered as he got out of his car, and walked briskly forward towards the house, to keep from falling.

He had become more of an adolescent child than a husband. His younger sister had committed suicide a few years ago, and she worried that he was also suicidal. And because of his health and heart condition, she also worried and wondered when she would wake up to find him dead.

"We had been so good together once." Tara whispered aloud. But now, she already looked forward to his leaving.

She had forgotten about the text from Tommy the moment Michael's car had turned in the drive. She needed to go inside. His presence caused her life to become even more difficult. She wouldn't allow her girls to be alone with him; it was another one of her rules. And she needed to make sure he hadn't fallen or done anything stupid on his way to his room.

She had allowed Hope and Heather to stay up all night last night watching old movies, and a Harry Potter Marathon. It was all part of their no-school-summer-ritual; a name she had made up to make it sound fun for her kids. Her disadvantage had made it impossible for them to go places that were non-accessible, so pizza delivery and slumber parties at home became their coup de grace. She knew they would both still be fast asleep, but she needed to be sure they were safe.

After ten minutes of fighting her way on two wheels through the grass, Tara made it to the ramp on her back porch and rolled smoothly up it. The back door was sitting wide open as her dogs lay in the comfortable shade on the porch. She went inside to check on Michael, but he was nowhere to be found.

"He must have gone upstairs and crashed." She thought.

Heather, her youngest, was sprawled out on the pull-out sofa bed in their vaulted-ceiling living room, in a one-piece pair of fuzzy blue pajamas, while Hope slept in her own room, nearly naked on the top bunk. Tara couldn't seem to keep clothes on that girl.

Hope was the child she worried most about. Walking around completely naked didn't bother her. It hadn't since she was a baby. She was fourteen years old now and had a thin fashion-model type build, but she still felt no shame whatsoever, walking around inside or out completely naked and unclothed. She didn't feel a need for clothes unless she was going to school or to a dance.

At home, she would walk around butt-ass-naked all the time if Tara didn't stay after her.

While both of her girls had blonde hair and blue eyes, Hope was the most striking to look at. She was also incredibly inexperienced about the ways of the world and men.

Most people might find Tara's way of raising children distasteful. But because of the way she had been abused as a child, she wanted her girls to know the truth about their world and their bodies despite what anyone might think of her. For example, she had explained to them what a "blow-job" was when they were in the sixth grade. She had also demonstrated how to give one to a boy effectively. This didn't mean that she approved of them having oral sex or otherwise, just that she wanted them to have the knowledge and wisdom of what sex was when they were old enough and ready to explore that kind of relationship.

She believed Hope, her oldest daughter, was already having intimate relations with her boyfriend. She had been dating him over the past two summers. He was

84

athletic and very handsome for his age. He was also a football player at their local high school, and he had been spending a lot of time with her at school and here at home, on the weekends.

She had noticed a change in their interactions one night as they lay together on the couch in the living room watching television. And ever since, Ben had been catering to Hope's every whim. Tara had been young once, too. She remembered the feelings, the passions and the warning signs.

Heather was the mischievous one of the two. She was thirteen years old. She was very smart like her father and had developed crafty ways to manipulate situations to her advantage. She also had the ability to lie, so well and with such an ingenious and soothing tongue, that she could charm a Grand Jury into believing her innocence.

Although she could be very convincing, she would be the first to acknowledge her own insecurities. It was difficult for her to trust her feelings as well as those of others. Her playful interactions with other girls had caused her to question her own desires and sexual orientations.

"What in the hell is going on." Michael yelled from the kitchen holding the door to the refrigerator open. "I told you to buy the food I liked. And where is my fucking beer?"

Tara jumped at the sound of his voice, as did the dogs and her girls. She rolled her chair into the kitchen immediately with a pale expression of concern on her face. Once again, after weeks of being away, his first words to her had been in anger.

"There's a case of beer under the cabinet." She said in a hushed tone as she pointed to the lower cabinets beside him. "And what would you like to eat? I'll fix you anything you want."

"I don't fucking want nothing." He answered as he slammed the refrigerator door.

His eyes were glassy and blank in appearance. He was only able to keep himself standing up by leaning against the counter; his legs wobbled because of his intoxicated state. He straightened his stance as he turned away from her, and he walked red-faced to the stairs that led to his room.

Michael was a good guy, his wife had told him so, and he had once loved her very much. But he had been banished to the upstairs rooms of his own home nearly a decade ago. And Tara hadn't touched him in well over ten years.

It had been even longer since he had been allowed to touch her. And she was his wife. It wasn't the same loving relationship they had once had, and it angered him.

She had isolated him, and he had begun to hate her.

She gave him no say in the raising of his own children and she treated him as though he were a stranger in his own house. And although he provided all the resources for his family, he received no respect from any of them.

So, he drank. He drank frequently, and he drank heavily.

And he hoped that one day soon, he would no longer awaken from his stoned, fucking nightmare of a life, having finally been drowned in the alcohol.

"I fucking hate it here!" Michael shouted as he turned and faced Tara sitting in her chair.

"Why are you here then?" She answered him coldly and just as loud. She couldn't remember the last time she had seen him sober.

"I wish you would divorce him, Mom." a high-pitched and shrilled voice screamed from behind them. They turned instantly to find Heather standing in the kitchen doorway in her pajamas. She had been there, watching and listening the whole time. "I wish you would just make him leave!" She screamed.

Michael picked up a vase filled with flowers from the breakfast nook beside him and threw it angrily against the opposing kitchen wall. It shattered with a crash as it burst into broken pieces of glass scattering all over the freshly cleaned hardwood floor.

Water and wet flowers were splashed all over the room.

Tara screamed maniacally.

The dogs barked crazily.

And emotions ran insanely high, as Hope walked up and wrapped her arms around Heather and stood in the kitchen doorway with her and cried.

TONY NALLEY

THE DARKNESS IN THE LIGHT

Chapter Eight – Strawberry Wine

Alongside an off-ramp, by a lamp post light outside of
Lawrenceburg, heading east on Highway thirty-one,
Tommy pulled to the shoulder and picked up a military
vet, who was thumbing a ride. The cardboard sign he
held read Cleveland, though it was misspelled, because
he could not read.

As he drove, the old man told him of his life; about the
women he had loved and of his children he didn't know.

He let him talk while he listened. It helped them both
ease their minds. He drove as far as the turnpike in Olive
Hill, exit one-twenty-one, off highway sixty-four,
because he was headed the other way.

"Thank you kindly, sir." The old man said as he shook
his hand and climbed out of the seat.

Tommy palmed him a twenty-dollar bill as he shook his
hand and gave him a pack of smokes.

"I appreciate the ride." The old man said with a tear in
his eye. "And may God bless you, my friend."

"God bless you too. And thank you for your service."
Tommy replied. "It's not much, but it might be enough to
get you through."

They waved to one another as Tommy flipped on his
blinker and re-entered the highway.

THE DARKNESS IN THE LIGHT

"It is strange." He thought. "How strangers become friends along a dark and lonesome road."

By the light of a crescent moon, he crossed into Ashton.

The straight stretch of highway could be traversed without headlights but for the oncoming traffic headed west. The heavens shined with glimmering starlight upon the whole of the world, or so it appeared as the hills and the trees of West Virginia came into view.

He didn't know the reason he had to leave. But he couldn't find a reason to stay. He hadn't heard from Tara in weeks. She hadn't texted back. So, he found himself lost on a highway, somewhere between heaven and hell, where the roads both led to her.

The rolling hills and wood of the Allegheny Mountains dampened the radio reception as their outlines blackened the sky, so he clicked off the car's stereo and drove in silence. He no longer had to concentrate his focus on the upcoming exit signs or turning lanes, because the way was straight and clear.

But the flashing yellow light on his dashboard indicated his tank was low, so he took the next exit and pulled into a station, to get some fuel.

As his pupils adjusted to the contrast of the gas station's blinding lights, he got out and walked across the convenience stores parking lot. Realizing that he had been driving all night wearing his aviator's, he raised them to his forehead as he opened the glass door and stepped inside.

Bells jingled as he entered the lobby, calling his attention to the young girl who stood at the counter.

She couldn't have been more than twenty-one. He was more than twice her age. She had long black hair pulled back into a ponytail and she greeted him with a smile and a hint of longing as he walked in.

He could see her tattooed half-sleeve through the whites of her shirt pulled down to her mid-forearm, underneath her red station vest. She was pretty. He was lonely. So, they talked for a while.

She was a first-year student in college. She was studying to become a nurse. She had gotten her GED after having her baby. And now that her little girl was old enough for preschool, she was continuing her education to better her child's life. Her baby-daddy was no longer in the picture.

And she only worked here to pay the rent. Her name was Brandi. He thought of the country song. She was warm as a glass of brandy. She was sweet as strawberry wine.

"Wait Darlin', let me lock the doors and dim the lights." She said as Tommy kissed and nuzzled her neck, holding her passionately against the wall.

As the lights dimmed, he unbuttoned his shirt and slipped out of his boots.

93

He was a good-looking man and he felt much younger than he was and more virile than he ever had been.

Wearing his faded blue jeans and his long-sleeved opened shirt, Tommy personified masculinity.

He wasn't ripped by any means, but he was nicely cut, and eye-catching. The hair on his chest was manly, as was his neatly trimmed mustache and beard. He wasn't a ladies-man per say, but he was the kind of man that ladies wanted.

When the door lock clicked, he steadied himself as Brandi ran across the shiny polished floors barefooted, and jumped into his arms, wrapping her legs and feet around his waist. He carried her into a little room in the back as she kissed him, and he sat her down on the break room table as she unzipped his jeans.

It had been a long time since he had been with a woman he didn't know. It wasn't for lack of trying on their part; it was very hard for Tommy to trust.

He needed more in a relationship than sex. He needed an emotional connection, a bond. But the wisdom of his years had made him keenly aware of his spiritual need as well as his physical need for intimacy. It was not only a want and desire; it was an actual physical need. So, occasionally, he would let his guard down and allow himself to feel the fires of a new lover.

Tommy took her to the floor.

Later, as he pulled a Marlboro cigarette from its pack and lit a flame, he drove up the on-ramp at three-forty-five in the morning. She gave him her number and he said he would call. And he would if the need should arise. But they both knew the truth. They had lives to live. He hoped he had left her feeling better about her life, even if only for the night. And she hoped she would see him again.

With his tank filled with gas, and a cold sandwich and a diet soda sitting in a plastic bag on the passenger seat, Tommy sat back behind the wheel and smoked. There were miles to travel between them as the welcome sign came into view. It was illuminated upon the hill between the pines.

He hadn't seen his friend in almost a year. Work and family were the common excuses made. Though in truth, it was always about time. Having steady positions in the work environment and having families to feed left a person with little time to socialize, let alone visit routinely with friends who lived three-hundred-miles away. It wasn't intentional. It wasn't intended. It was life.

Seth and Tommy had been kids together. They met when they were in the fifth grade, in Mr. Chesser's liberal re-education class to undermine the US Constitution. Or so they would later come to believe. Seth was reading a comic book. Tommy wasn't. Even as a child, Tommy didn't care for comic books, although he would later develop an appetite for the Guardians of the Galaxy movies.

When they were in the seventh grade, Seth and his family moved away to Vicars, West Virginia, to be closer to his mom's side of the family, after his parents had gotten divorced. But until then, Seth and Tommy had been inseparable. They formed their own club; they became generals of their own private armies, and they created secrets to guard, war games to play and flags to capture.

They were best friends.

The darkened car's interior suddenly glowed brightly with a burst of light.

Tommy's cell phone resounded with a loud ding, from somewhere in the passenger seat beside him. As his eyes adjusted to the contrast, Tommy reached for his phone and his attention left the highway.

"HONNNNNK..." The horn resounded. Tommy swerved instantly to the right as the oncoming diesel's horn blew. "HONK... HONNNNK..." The horn resounded again.

The light refraction from its headlights nearly blinded him. He shielded his eyes with his forearm and prayed that no one was in front or behind him.

"DAMN IT TO HELL." Tommy shouted.

"HONNNNNK..." The driver of the eighteen-wheeler blew his horn one final time. And with a rush of wind, a squeal of tires and a ghost of reprieve it had barely missed him..

"Fuck! Fuck! Fuck! Fuck!" He said aloud as he slapped the steering wheel. "I almost fucked it all up right there."

Tommy's heart thumped profusely within his chest as he brought his car back under control and into his right lane.

And he breathed a deep sigh of relief that he hadn't just shit himself.

With eyes wide open, he signaled and pulled over to the side of the road. The way was black. There was no one around who would see his blinker, but he turned it on anyway.

He stepped out upon shaking legs, into the grass just off the highway, and took a long and much needed piss. After he'd zipped up, Tommy walked back to his car and sat down upon the hood. And he lit up another smoke.

As he looked out at the stars, he thought of her. He hadn't thought of her for hours. He hadn't heard from her in weeks. And now suddenly, out of the starlit sky, her timing had almost cost him his life.

He read her message. And then he stuffed his phone into the back-pocket of his jeans.

He smiled between blowing smoke and chuckling to himself because he had thought of something funny.

"I cleared my mind of Tara, while Brandi cleared my pipes." He said it aloud.

97

He thought it was funny, though it sounded funnier in his mind.

In the stillness of the night, he continued driving and he laughed as the music from the Eagles gently played.

♫ Well, I'm running down the road, trying to loosen my load. I've got seven women on my mind. Four that want to own me, two that want to stone me, and one says she's a friend of mine. Take It easy, take it easy. Don't let the sound of your own wheels drive you crazy. Lighten up while you still can. Don't even try to understand. Just find a place to make your stand and take it easy. ♫

THE DARKNESS IN THE LIGHT

Chapter Nine – Tabernacle of the Holy

Their plane touched down in the middle of a pouring rain, at three-twenty-two in the morning, eastern daylight time. Tara peered out through the window as most of the other passengers slept. The lights upon their landing shone brightly through the glass as they reflected upon the waters that fell onto the runway.

The storm had raged since their departure from Philadelphia International Airport, on their crossover flight to Boston.

She had made reservations for three days and four nights, at a little Bed and Breakfast in Cambridge. The brochure painted a pretty picture of pink lace and periwinkle, with polished hardwood floors and handmade quilts. It had separate entrances, porches, and a garden. And it was set back from the street at the end of a garden path. It was located within an historic district that personified the valor of fallen soldiers of the American Revolution, within walking distance of local cemeteries filled with ghosts and spirits of times long past.

Tara had traveled the world over. After her car accident, she pursued higher education at a major University and had earned a degree in Psychology. She had also worked for local and major radio stations to make her way and pay for her education. Her chance meetings with people of affluence had led her from there to work in industries that dedicated their engineering capabilities to the design and coordination of equipment, for the disabled. And being disabled herself, her quick wit and steadfast determination had allowed her to use her abilities to rapidly move up into the upper epsilon of management.

She had a pretty face. And everyone loved her. They loved her immediately and they loved her completely. She had a certain way about her. She was contagious, enticing, and illusive. She was more than just a pretty face that brightened the room when she entered.

Somehow, she created an instant bond the moment she'd lock eyes with you. She could make you believe you were the most important person she'd ever known. The feeling was euphoric, mesmerizing and be-witching.

It was a girls-only-getaway-weekend. She had planned it that way. She deliberately penciled in times and dates on her day-planner, that directly correlated with the times and dates her husband, Michael, would be home.

Tara's home was her sanctuary, her refuge. And his violent mood swings and childish manner, coupled with his unyielding pursuit of death by alcoholism, disrupted it. So, she pursued harmony in the subtle nuances of travel. She found solace in the distance.

She had the driver pick them up at the airport. The girls slept comfortably on the opposing leather seats once they had climbed into the shelter of the stretch, while Tara slowly concocted a mixture of Maraschino Liqueur from the complimentary cocktail bar. It wasn't often that she allowed herself the luxury of a chauffeured limousine, but she did have the money. She had only recently transferred funds to cover Michael's monthly seven-thousand-dollar credit card payment. She wasn't hurting.

She had long since passed the time when she had worried about having the money to pay the rent or the electricity.

But she didn't like to be wasteful either.

Tara had an advanced sense of taste and smell. Her drink tasted sweet and smelled of spring cherries. She remembered the smell of cherries on the tree …and of honeysuckles on the vine.

"Tommy had always loved how I smelled of honeysuckles." She thought.

She had forgotten to text him. Her last few weeks had been maddening.

She sat her drink down as they rode and took out her iPhone. It was four-seventeen in the morning.

"Are you planning anything fun for next weekend?" She texted him; she knew he wouldn't respond right away. It was too late or way too early, depending upon whichever way you wanted to look at it.

"If he asks where I am, I'll tell him we're fugitives on the lam." She laughed to herself. And then she thought about it further and began to chuckle to herself.

"I'll tell him I've sold my girls into prostitution." Tara was laughing so hard she spilled her drink in the seat. "Yes. Yes. And I'll tell him Hope's a topless dancer at the T&A strip club and gets twenty guys a night."

Tara laughed aloud.

"I'll …I'll …I'll tell him Heather is making porn at the local prison." She thought as she cackled so hard she nearly lost her breath. "And that she's just trying to do her part to show love to underprivileged minorities."

With that …Tara burst out laughing hysterically.

She knew her sense of humor was dark and twisted. It always had been.

It was part of her charm.

She thought it was hilarious. And she laughed openly as the driver glanced back at her through the limo's rear-view mirror. She pushed the little button and closed the dark glass partition between them while she took another sip of her drink. And she laughed some more.

The driver was a large Black man whose name, she would later learn, was James. He stood as tall as he was wide, and he had a wonderfully white and welcoming smile. He drove for his brother-in-law, who owned the business and was highly successful. His sister had married well. James wasn't married, nor did he have children. He lived a bachelors' life, though not by choice.

He had been in love once. She had died of cancer. He would never get over her.

James pulled the car onto a private circular driveway, around to a well-designed and fully accessible welcome entrance, at the Bed and Breakfast Inn. It was lovely, albeit what she could see of it through the dark and the rain. It was pink. It had lights.

He brought her chair around to her door and offered her his gentlemanly assistance, as he sheltered her from the rain with a large, open umbrella, and she fearlessly climbed in.

Her wheelchair was specifically designed by one of her companions from the engineering firm she had one time managed. It had a smooth and slim frame that was congruent to racing chairs. There were no handles on its back. She thought chairs with handles made them look like handicapped chairs. She wasn't handicapped. She was physically challenged. Her chair looked sleek and almost sexy. And she felt sexy in it.

After they had weathered the storm and checked into the lobby, James carried their luggage to their room, and then he said his goodbyes for the night. The girls crashed wherever they landed, Heather on the couch, Hope on a pillow on the floor beside her. Tara felt she could sleep for days.

When she found the comfort of her bed, she slept for twenty-four hours.

She awakened to the sounds of children laughing and playing. Hope and Heather had been watching movies all day in the living room and had created their own private party out of the food and the drinks and the ice cream they had ordered. They had managed to remember to plug their iPhones into their chargers, but the room was a mess. And they sat in the middle of it, cross-legged and barefoot on the floor.

Tara checked her iPhone. Tommy hadn't messaged her back.

But there had been a call from PJ.

She had dated PJ briefly after her accident. Though he wasn't the usual kind of guy she would typically date. He was, however, the first guy she had dated, who hadn't known her prior to her accident, when her spinal cord had been severely injured. He had never seen her walk. He had been good to her though, she remembered that. And they had kissed while they had dated in high school, but it was nothing serious. She didn't remember why they had broken up.

PJ was a good guy. She thought he was strong and handsome, though others had commented on his strange looking appearance. He was different, she would admit that. But it was his inability to comprehend the simplest of things that disheartened her. He couldn't read or write very well. He wasn't very well educated. He was the kind of person she normally tried to help psychologically.

106

Besides, he was married. And he had been married, to the same woman, since graduating from high school.

He had re-entered her life a month before he had escorted her to the party, where she had reconnected with Tommy.

And she had noticed soon thereafter that his truck passed by her house more frequently and on numerous occasions. At first, she thought it was coincidental. But it had become apparent that he was purposely making the detour along her road, to see if she was home or if anyone was in her driveway. She received calls from him regularly. And he became angry with her easily if she did not answer or return his calls in the amount of time he felt was appropriate.

Not only had his behavior revealed a stalker type personality, but he had also revealed a physically and verbally intrusive nature. With the fingers of his hand, he had attempted to violate her one afternoon, while simultaneously whispering in her ear that he wanted to rape her. Tara dismissed his conduct entirely; because she thought him to be a good guy and that he didn't mentally understand the depravity of his actions. She felt through her interactions and conversations with him, that he had been allowed to behave this way with others and had never been corrected for this manner of conduct.

He was her friend, and she didn't think of him otherwise. So, she felt, given her background in psychology, she could collaborate with him.

107

Tara pushed the button on her phone and dialed his number.

"About time." His voice chimed out through the speaker phone.

"Sorry, I've been asleep since we got here." Tara replied sleepily.

"My wife read your messages on my phone." He said distinctly. "She wants a divorce."

"What messages?" Tara asked.

"The ones from you," PJ stated, "And the pictures."

Tara couldn't remember anything that she would have or could have texted him that would lead his wife to believe she had anything but honorable intentions for her husband. She had told him specifically, and on numerous occasions, that she only wanted to be his friend and nothing more. However, she knew that he had other intents and purposes regarding her.

She also could not remember any pictures she may have sent him, that could be, in any way construed, as sensual or sexual by nature.

He didn't call her attention to them. But there they were.

He had the proof on his phone.

"I'm so sorry, PJ." Tara replied. "I'm sorry you're going through this."

"What are we going to do about it?" He asked.

"I don't know. What do you want me, I mean us, to do about it?" She asked.

"I don't know, but I'm losing my house and my wife and my kids over you." He stated. "I don't know what I'm going to do."

"Let's talk about it next weekend when I get home." Tara said. "We can sit down and work everything out then."

"Cool." He replied.

"Cool." Tara answered. "I'll talk with you then." She said as he hung up the phone.

Tara dismissed his call entirely from her mind. She didn't want her and her children's get-away to be dampened by another man's temperamental and erratic situation. They were on Retreat. This trip was their asylum. And she would not give rise to obvious attempts to disrupt their inner sanctum.

"Girls," Tara shouted. They both came running. "Do you want to go check out the graveyard?" She asked them.

"Yes." Hope said immediately as she jumped up and down excitedly while prayerfully clapping her hands together. She enjoyed the same kinds of things her mother enjoyed.

Heather was less excited than her sister was. She didn't like ghosts and spooky places. She watched scary movies, but she wasn't thrilled about visiting graveyards at night, where the monsters lived.

Tara loved anything, and everything related to spirits and the macabre. She prayed at the high altars of the paranormal and she enjoyed chilling journeys in the dead of night, in hopes of being made witness to strange or ghoulish encounters.

"Can I dance naked in the graveyard?" Hope asked. "Seriously, Mom, can I?"

Tara looked at her beautiful, blonde haired blue-eyed child and wondered what she was going to do with her.

She was a highly intelligent, creative, and talented, fourteen-year-old bundle of loveliness. But she often made her wonder if she could simultaneously be a special-needs child.

Truthfully, Tara found Hope's inhibitions refreshing.

And she liked that she was proud of her body. As a child she had felt inferior about her own. It was going to be dark soon. And if this was to be her daughters' pivotal moment, then damn it. She would allow her to dance naked in the graveyard.

At least she would be dancing upon consecrated ground, where no one could see her, instead of on a stripper pole in some sleazy nightclub. And she knew definitively that Hope would always remember her naked excursion through the cemetery. She would remember it for the rest of her life.

"Yes." Tara agreed. "But you're not going to be a stripper on a pole. No lap dances or turning tricks." She said jokingly. "And all child-porn is strictly forbidden." She said as she laughed and pointed her finger. "No suggestive or sensual pictures to shamelessly heighten your social media status either. None," she stated emphatically. "And wear your clothes until we get there. I don't want to be pulled over and arrested for the transportation of a naked underage minor. Get undressed under a coat or jacket once we get there."

"We didn't bring any, Mom." Her youngest daughter Heather replied.

"Check the bathroom closet." Tara answered. "There may be a robe or a large towel in there."

There was a robe. It was small, white, and it came to Hope's mid-thigh.

She looked like a Victoria Secrets model, only more youthful and innocent.

"You could definitely do porn." Her mom said to her.

Hope wouldn't mind.. She was proud of her body. And she enjoyed it. She was on the pill, and she really enjoyed pleasuring men.

Society would call her a whore or a slut no matter what she did, just because she was a female. If a guy had sex every day, his social stature would be elevated. He would be called a stud. Hope didn't care what people thought of her. She liked what she liked. And she also loved the pleasures.

Hope had been with her boyfriend, Ben, since she was twelve years old. But her mom didn't know, at least not the part of her mom that she called the light. Her mom's darkness knew. The darkness knew everything.

She hadn't understood the darkness when she was little, but she had come to realize and recognize the subtle change when it happened. It fell over her, much like a shadow. And the dynamic contrast changed her personality when it took control.

She named them separately, the light and the darkness, because there were two different sides of her mom.

Naming them was one of her rules.

The light was her mom's truest self. It was the side of her that was funny, amusing, and delightful. It was the goodness and light in her that did the normal everyday mom and daughter things. The light was also their

disciplinarian and their protector. The light was their
mom, their real mom.

The darkness was deviant, more of a sexual creature than
a mother. When her mom's light went out, she had no
memory of the darkness or of anything the darkness had
done. She recalled nothing from the moment it took her
over. And often, she would forget even more memories.

The darkness controlled what she could and could not
call to mind. And because of this, it allowed her to do
unspeakable things.

It had been this way all of Hope's life. She knew no other
normal. She had accepted her mothers' darkness and had
learned to use it for her own advantages and purposes.

Hope didn't obey or conform to the rules of social
moralities or societal standards. She had anyone she
wanted, however she wanted, whenever or wherever she
wanted, with whomever she wanted, and with how many
she wanted at the same time.

The darkness, that side of her mom, had allowed her and
had cultivated her to be this way. But she was burdened
by her fears of her mom being found out and locked
away in a mental institution for having done so. She was
afraid and worried that she and her sister would be left
alone with their father. He was a stranger to them. He
was more of a spoiled older brother who told them what
to do, than a real dad. She didn't know him. She didn't
like him. And she didn't trust him, because she was smart

enough to know lust, when she saw it in a grown man's eyes.

Hope and Heather barely remembered last night's drive from the airport, so they were extremely thrilled with the chauffeured limousine, as James drove them to the cemetery.

They liked James. They thought he was funny.

They bounced on the seats. They turned all the dials.

They pushed all the buttons.

And then they stood up, through the limo's open sunroof, and excitedly waved and shouted at passersby. Tara liked seeing them happy. They had grown almost immune to joy.

And she hoped they were keeping their tops on.

She read a message from Tommy as she sat comfortably in the back. It had come stealthily. She hastily replied.

"Hey baby. I'm sorry. I had been getting the girls and me ready for this vacation. We're in Boston. You and I catching up is just a given. Period." Tara texted.

"Saturday night was like no time had passed. I love that. I love you. And I will talk to you soon." Hugs, Kisses, Hugs, Kisses, Hugs emojis were added. "Are you still coming to my party on the seventh?" She texted further.

114

"Hope you enjoy your vacation." Tommy replied. "I'm good for the party. We're lifelong friends, that'll never change. Please call. I was worried about you." Tommy continued. "I'm here. I'm a pretty good listener, too. I've got your back."

"Thank you. You have no idea how much that means to me." Tara responded. "I could seriously use an anchor about now. You've always been a calming presence, which pairs well with my 'Jo-Jo the idiot circus boy' side. Which I am experiencing a lot of here lately."

"Life happens …emotions run rampant. I thought that would end after I was younger." Tommy replied. "Nope, we still have to control them and guard our hearts, because our hearts can't see past love."

"I saw past it a long time ago. Now it's just about self-preservation. It's still a very unstable situation that changes moment by moment and you never know what's coming, or when it's really safe to come out. That's why our reunion was such a big deal for me. It was the first thing I'VE done that didn't involve using my girls as a cover …in ten years." Tara related. "I've gotten years invested in planning a getaway that can't be planned, if that makes sense."

"I'm here. I'm your friend. I expect nothing. I ask for nothing." Tommy replied. "You need me …night or day, I'm here. You've got a friend – James Taylor."

"I love that," replied Tara. "Please, please …just say a lot of nice, kind, respectful, supportive words to me. I'll follow you around forever." She continued. "To quote one of my favorite movies, 'A gentlemen …I almost forgot what you guys look like'."

As the car pulled alongside a large metal fence linked together tightly, with large arrow shaped spikes aligning each bar, Tara said goodbye to Tommy and she and Hope quickly got out.

The darkened outline was unnerving, as James leaned heavily against the side of the limousine. He stood watch as Tara rolled slowly upon the paved and murky walkways of the old stone cemetery.

She called out to the spirits by name, as she read them from their epitaphs by the bright of the moon's light. Heather sat safely inside the long of the car, looking out through its shaded glass, as Hope removed her clothing and walked barefoot upon the grass.

She appeared like a ghost, a shimmering child of mist, as she danced beneath the starlight.

And as she danced and played, Tara captured an image of her on her iPhone.

The scene was too surreal, and too beautiful, to remain sight unseen.

Tara watched her teenage daughter dance betwixt the ancient stones.

She was enlightened, unashamed and naked amidst the moonlight.

This was her freedom, her shrine, her tabernacle of the Holy.

And Tara let her dance.

THE DARKNESS IN THE LIGHT

Chapter Ten – We Really Didn't Go to the Moon

He was twenty-two when he saw his first Lynyrd Skynyrd concert. They played LIVE and on stage at the Lexington Rupp Arena. He found it hard to concentrate, with the smoking hot sixteen-year-old girl he had brought with him, sitting beside him, pleasing him in the stands.

Her name was Sarah. She spelled it with an H. She was innocently seductive. And her eyes were emerald, green.

She was a gorgeous creature with darkly flowing hair and incredibly voluptuous boobs. They were firm and soft. She loved flaunting them at him, as well as showing off her smooth sun-tanned legs, while wearing her faded cut-off jeans. Tommy loved watching her walk. But he loved her kisses more.

While his attention and his lips were deeply focused on Sarah's fire, he did vaguely remember the band taking the stage through multi-colored lights, and he faintly recalled hearing them play Freebird.

"I think the opening band was The Four Horseman." Tommy said to his friend Seth. "The rest is kind of fuzzy."

"Molly Hatchet. That's the band. You need to see them in concert." Seth replied, "Amazing."

Tommy rested as he rocked back and forth on the covered back porch swing, watching the smoke from the fires of the bar-b-que grill. The screened porch was secluded …off the side of the house, facing outwards into the trees.

The steaks sizzled over the open fire as the wind blew briskly.

Seth cooked the most amazing and the absolute best rib-eye steaks he'd ever eaten. He used chips of cherry wood to stoke the flame, as he carefully seasoned the meat with secret salts and peppers. The seared steaks were caramelized on the outside, while remaining juicy in the middle. A knife wasn't needed; you could eat them with a fork.

Life seemed simpler and more peaceful in West Virginia. Seth's home sat upon an embankment above a winding creek, surrounded by tall pines and evergreens. The wind whisked through the leaves bringing with it the smells of native flowers and the freshness of the cool mountain air.

"Okay, so tell me about this woman." Seth said as he popped open a Bud-light. "You said her name was, Tara?"

"You may remember her." Tommy replied. "She shared the same classes in elementary school, between the fifth and seventh grades. She's the one I've spoken with you about hundreds of times." Tommy continued. "I kissed her for the first time under a Christmas Tree. Remember?"

"I don't remember meeting her. But I remember you telling me about her." Seth replied. "The only girls I remember from back then were named Bobbie and Donna. Bobbie reminded me of Leather Tuscadero from the television hit show called Happy Days. And Donna, well, she looked more like Sandra Dee from the John Travolta movie Grease."

"Olivia Newton John, yes, she did. You're right." Tommy stated. "You know? Donna died in a traffic accident in Boston a few years back. She was married and had two children; I believe. And Bobbie is still single, I hear she's still a wild rebel child."

"Did you fuck her?" Seth asked slyly.

"Who? Bobbie? Hell No." Tommy stated. "We were kids. I don't even remember talking to her. She was a tough little chic. I wasn't as bad ass as I am now." He finished, emphasizing his manly prowess.

"Dude, no. I mean Tara." Seth corrected. "Have you fucked Tara?"

"Does a gentleman say yes or no to that question?" Tommy answered quickly.

"Fuck all that, man. Tell me about it." Seth replied attentively. "Did you fuck her?" He said accentuating each word separately.

"We've been together twice." Tommy answered, "Once, in the backseat of a car; driving home from a rock concert, when we were both fifteen-years-old." He said. "And once again, about three weeks ago, by a candle's light in a little room in the dark."

"You're fucked." Seth stated emphatically. "You know? I've been saying, fuck, a lot. I'm going to stop."

"You're screwed, Dude." He started again correcting his language as he laughed.

Tommy sat back in the swing and lit up a cigarette. And then he took a drink from his wine glass.

"She's married, man. And she's got two girls, right?" Seth asked. "And this is her second marriage?"

"She's currently married to her third husband. And Yes." Tommy said as he nodded. "Heather and Hope, ages thirteen and fourteen."

"It's a hornet's nest, brother." Seth implied emphatically. "I believe you care about her. But she's not what you need. She's going to chew you up and spit you out. I'm not trying to hurt you, and no matter what, it's your life and I'll support whatever decision you make. But no matter how beautiful she is and no matter how great you are together, the rose-colored glasses you're wearing are going to come off soon, and you're going to find yourself in a world of shit."

"Don't hold back, brother." Tommy said laughing. "Tell me how you really feel."

"DAMN IT. I forgot to turn the steaks." Seth said as he jumped up from his chair and hurriedly reached over the flames and turned the meat on the grill.

The sounds were inviting and the smell as they cooked was delicious. Smoke and steam poured out into the open air. And the sight of Seth almost spilling his beer, as he messed with the fire, was hilarious.

Tommy didn't come to visit his friend to get advice about Tara. Though, he knew he would get some, whether he wanted to or not. He came to get away and to clear his mind. He came to shoot the shit and have some drinks with his best friend and have some fun. He knew before he left for home, that they would have exhausted all avenues of discussion, concerning politics, current events, UFO and Dog-man sightings as well as the even more lengthy topics, such as their philosophies on the real-life Matrix and their Flat Earth theories.

"You know we really didn't go to the moon." Seth said sullenly. "It's all a giant hoax perpetrated by the Nazi regime after World War II when we brought their scientists to the US and formed NASA."

"Did we really win the war?" Tommy asked knowing where the conversation would lead, "World War II?"

"We may have won it militarily and for all intents and purposes regarding wars up until that time. It appeared to the world that we had won. But we really didn't. The Nazi's propaganda machine was so ingrained and so proficient that it continues to be used against the American public and against Christians around our circular plane to this day." Seth lamented. He knew Tommy was directing the conversation with his questions. But he enjoyed being able to converse on so many distinct levels with someone who shared his same beliefs.

Seth was a Christian. He was not the kind you would find at the local church on Sunday morning, after a wild night out on the town that Saturday night. His belief was not on display for others to think better of him. His belief in God was built upon a firm and solid foundation. He believed Jesus Christ was his Lord and Savior. And he believed that God had sent His Son, Jesus, to die for our sins and be raised again unto His glory.

Seth also believed in several things that, when vomited out too quickly in the middle of a conversation with someone who was not as well educated in the truth, would lead anyone to believe he was out of his mind.

"The Liberals and the Main-Stream Media have such a strangle hold upon the mindset of this country, that if you say anything they don't agree with, they will brandish you a racist, a Nazi sympathizer or a UFO nut-job wearing a tin foiled hat to keep the CIA from infiltrating their mind." Seth said in entirety without taking a breath.

"This world is going to shit, man. Thank God Trump won the Presidency. Baby-killer Hillary would have handed us over on a silver platter."

Tommy took another drink of wine. It tasted sweet, though a little tart. And he listened to his friend while lighting up another smoke.

"They say they're open-minded. But they're not. If you don't believe the same ways they do, then they try to shut you up. And that's when they label you publicly as a bigot, a homophobe, a racist or a Nazi. Hell, look it up. Hitler was a socialist. Fascism encompassed a dictatorial doctrine of hatred and murder crimes across most of the world. He murdered millions. And his madness didn't stop with the murder of Jews. He killed anybody and everybody who stood in his way. He killed homosexuals, liberal union members and bosses, women and children. There is no way they should have the right to compare Hitler's regime to the current US Conservative party. There's no way." Seth continued.

"They call what they do as it fits their agenda. Burning an effigy of a conservative president hanging from a tree is deemed as an expression of ART. And they claim it's a protected right under the Second Amendment of the US Constitution." He took a breath and lit up a smoke.

"While legally and peacefully protesting and voicing conservative opinions that are in direct contrast to a sitting President, who just so happens to be half-black, his mamma was white, is considered racist." Seth took a breath. "It blows my FREAKING MIND."

Tommy lit up another cigarette.

"It's all controlled by George Soros." Seth continued. "And he was in the Nazi SS during Hitler's reign. Remember that the next time the George Soros funded Liberals call you a racist, fascist or Nazi."

Tommy's phone lit up and vibrated on his lap. It was a message from Tara.

"She's naked with ghosts in a graveyard in Boston?" He read her note twice to understand, but he was still perplexed.

"I don't know how to respond to that." He thought as he placed his phone on the swings cushion beside him. Then he picked it back up and texted, "Okay." And then he put it back down.

"Was that a text from her?" Seth asked.

"Yes." Tommy answered.

"Is she the girl you kept the secret for?" Seth asked. "Is she the girl in that church in Indiana?"

"Michigan." Tommy corrected.

"Oh my God. Oh my God." Seth said as he sat back in his chair by the door, laid the back of his head against the brick wall, and stared up at the ceiling. "I understand now, brother. I understand." He said calmly as he looked back towards his friend.

"You know that I am a medical nurse for Brooke Dale Hospital, it's a psych ward and I've been in the medical field for a number of years." He said as Tommy nodded, yes. "I worked on the psych floor for almost four years, and believe me when I say, that I've seen and heard a lot of unspeakable things. I worked with children who had suffered terrible abuses, psychological abuses, physical and sexual abuses. And I've even worked with patients who were children themselves when they committed crimes against other children, severely." Seth said as Tommy listened tentatively.

"What happens to the emotional and mental state of a child when they suffer from a traumatic event, is that a defensive mechanism is enabled in their subconscious. Boys and girls process trauma differently. Little boys tend to act out in anger, often violently. They can develop sociopathic tendencies, as they disconnect themselves from their feelings; little girls, especially girls under the age of thirteen or fourteen-years-old, bury their feelings and emotions deep within their psychological make up, often resulting in a split personality. These personalities take control and are often awakened by abusive situations, overtly sexual situations. They may not even be aware of it happening and will suffer from blackouts and memory loss. And the loss of memory is

127

beyond what would be explained by ordinary forgetfulness." He continued. "One personality becomes their protector. It will defend and shelter their natural personality from any form of harm. That's how they can wake up, not knowing where their bruises or wounds came from."

Tommy believed his best friend assumed he was innocent, and unaware of the evils of the world. And he felt he had to remind him often, that, even though he cherished innocence above most all other human values, his innocent side was part of his charm. He was very aware of issues regarding the dark side of humanity.

"I am also concerned for her two daughters, man." Seth continued. "They are ages thirteen and fourteen, right? They've been raised in an environment where their mother's separate identities and possible sociopathic behaviors, are the only normal they have ever known." Seth continued. "Even if it hasn't caused them to act out highly sexually, possibly with an insatiable appetite, they will be defensive of her and their family's perception of what is normal, to them."

Seth knew his best friend very well. He was one of the brightest and most intelligent people he had ever known, but he sometimes wondered if he grasped the entire meaning of his words.

"You're a man of your word." He said as he leaned over and looked Tommy straight in the eye. "You'd keep your word, even if you had to break your leg doing it." He said. "This happened when you were how old? Fourteen?" He asked, and Tommy nodded. "You were a child. You were a fourteen-year-old boy who absolutely loved this beautiful young girl who you kissed under the lights of a Christmas tree." He continued.

"You loved her so much, that when you caught her with another guy, you didn't get angry. You didn't cry. You didn't push her away. You kept a promise to her. And you buried it in your heart. You buried a secret that she asked you to keep because you loved her. You bottled up all the emotional pain and trauma inside you. her secret was protecting the guy she was with, not you. He was an older man, and a youth Minister of the Church." Seth said and then drank the rest of his beer. "You knew something didn't feel right when you caught them together. But you had no way of knowing she was being abused by a child predator, a pedophile."

Tommy didn't respond. He didn't have the words.

"I know you are in-love with her, brother, but you're in-love with the fourteen-year-old girl she once was, not the woman she is now. The fourteen-year-old boy inside of you is still in-love with her, not the grown man you are now. Do you understand?" Seth asked. Tommy nodded.

"There is a high probability that Tara has developed a multiple personality disorder." Seth continued as he returned to his normal tone. "Though, it's now more commonly referred to as Dissociative Identity Disorder."

Then he turned to his friend sympathetically and with feeling.

"It's a wonder you didn't explode, Tommy." Seth stated. "This was a life shattering and traumatic event that happened. I'm surprised you didn't develop some form of sociopathic tendencies or a split in personalities yourself, causing you to act out violently."

"Remember the girl I was seeing a couple of years ago, who ran off with that guy, and left me struggling with depression for months?" Tommy asked.

"Yes, I remember." Seth answered. "We had multiple conversations at length regarding that situation.

"You don't hear me talking about her anymore, right?" He asked, and Seth shook his head, no, remembering that he had not.

"Can you keep a secret?" Tommy asked. Seth nodded, yes.

"I buried her with her boyfriend under a concrete slab in an affluent neighborhood in Bedford. The construction was new and still under development, and the foundation was scheduled to be poured the morning I murdered and disposed of their bodies." Tommy stated as a matter of fact.

Then, he sat backward upon the swing, stone faced and devoid of expression.

Seth's jaw dropped.

He reviewed Tommy's facial expressions for any sign of change. And he continued to stare into the eyes of his best friend questioningly, for what seemed to be an enormous amount of time.

And then Tommy broke a smile.

"You mother fucker." Seth exclaimed. "Damn it to Hell you motherfucker. You got me." He said at last. "You mother-fucking got me."

Tommy chuckled and smiled like a Cheshire cat, as he drank the last of the wine from his glass and lit up another cigarette.

"You scared the fuck out of me right there, brother." Seth said as he laughed and patted him on his shoulder.

Then he stood up from his chair and walked to the grill.

"Steaks are served Brother." He said. "Let's eat."

THE DARKNESS IN THE LIGHT

Chapter Eleven – The Ritual of Lights

Down a one-lane winding road, outlined on either side by thick wood and tall grass, Tommy drove cautiously. The curved roadway was marked by a high circular mirror, attached to a cedar telephone pole, to view the occurrence of oncoming vehicles more easily around the bend. It led to a straighter stretch of highway that crossed a flowing creek, by way of a low-lying cream-colored concrete bridge.

As the thoroughfare divided to the right and to the left, he turned his wheel and traveled for miles without meeting a single car coming from either direction. Within minutes of realizing he had made a wrong turn; he quickly turned the car around and made a corrected left.

Tara's beautiful home came into view shortly thereafter, upon a field of grassy green. It sat at the end of a long-graveled driveway filled with many cars and trucks, and was marked by red, white, and blue balloons tied to her mailbox.

Tommy's heart raced with anticipation. He hadn't met Tara's husband. And he was poised for him to be there. Although he was unsure of how their first conversation would begin, he was confident that he could handle any form of confrontation they might have, in a calm and positive manner.

This would also be his first introduction to her girls, Hope and Heather. He was more concerned about

133

meeting them. Being a father himself, he knew they were more important than any other persons in Tara's life.

He wanted to make a good first impression.

As he parked and walked up the drive, Michael met and greeted him by the garage doors, and shook his hand firmly.

"I've heard a lot of good things about you." Michael said. "I hear you and Tara are going to be working together. She's excited about writing again. It'll be good for her."

Tara had spoken with Tommy briefly about writing, but it had been placed on the back burner once they had fallen into one another's arms. She had a knack for writing and had published articles for magazines and collective works that had been on the New York Times Best Seller's List. While he had published five books of his own and had also put out a CD of his written songs, he looked forward to the synergy, and the innovation they would create together.

Tara's girls ran through the grass excitedly, and soaking wet, as they playfully chased their friends.

Michael yelled to them as they entered the pool. He called them over, and he introduced them to Tommy.

"Girls, this is the guy your mom talked about." He said. "He's going to be here a lot. He'll be working with your mom."

Hope walked up to Tommy, shiny and dripping wet, and held open her arms for him. Tommy reminded himself of her age, as he turned his eyes away and reached out for her embrace.

"Welcome to our home." Hope said. "We've been looking forward to meeting you. You make our mom happy and that makes us happy." She said sweetly and then she lightly kissed him on the cheek.

Hope found Tommy extremely attractive, tall and becoming.

She couldn't find a glint of lust in his eyes when he looked at her, but she did feel a shimmer of longing, when she had pressed herself tightly against his body.

She had been with several of her mom's guy friends, before she had hooked up with Ben. When her mom's darkness took over, she could do whatever she wanted, and she had.

It had been a while since her boyfriend Ben had stimulated her. She would send him home early tonight, after the fireworks.

Then she could light her own fireworks. She wanted him.

Tommy turned to embrace Heather as she came in for a wet hug as well. And as he stood moistly between her soaking wet children, Tara rolled down the sidewalk and motioned him to greet her too. So, he let loose her girls, bent over and embraced her, pulling her in close.

Tara was overly excited to see Tommy arrive. Though, she was also fearful of her husband Michael's reactions to him, and of his recent alarming behaviors towards her and her girls.

He had become increasingly verbally abusive since their return from Boston. His temperament had become more unstable, when mixed with his alcohol, and had rapidly escalated into physical abuse.

She wore the badges upon her legs and arms, of slowly fading bruises.

Heather watched her mom as she hugged this complete and total stranger.

She knew her mom was sleeping with him. She could tell by the way her eyes sparkled whenever she spoke of him, and she could see why. He was a very handsome and attractive older man.

Her sister noticed, too. And she could tell her sister was going to sleep with him, too. And it made her angry because she was tired of being left out. She was tired of being the baby.

Heather and Hope were best friends. They were close and they shared everything with one another, even their boyfriends. She had been aware of the darkness and the light in their mother, from as far back as she could remember. And she knew everything that Hope knew; at least she believed she did. She was also keenly aware of her sisters' more ravenous sexual escapades.

Hope had allowed her to watch her and her boyfriend once. Heather found it stimulating. Ben had been inebriated, and Hope had let her touch him. She liked the way he moved. And she enjoyed his excitement.

While she stood beside her sister, Heather was torn between her visions and what was currently happening right in front of their father.

He knew nothing.

He was oblivious.

He was lost and disconnected.

She pitied him.

"I'm making a beer and ice run." Michael said. "Anyone want to ride?"

No one volunteered. So, Michael went out alone.

Tommy was happy about how well his introductions had been. As the girls returned to their water-games, Tara went inside to freshen up. And he was left to make polite conversation with the other guests.

Tommy spoke with her friend PJ outside beneath a shade tree, as he held a cold Bud Light and smoked a cigarette.

He had been the guy who had escorted her the night he and Tara had been reunited. While she had stated emphatically that she and PJ were close friends and nothing more, he had witnessed their interactions. He wasn't stupid. And he could feel the tensions arise as he walked up and offered him his hand.

"My wife is divorcing me." PJ told him. "She found texts and pictures from Tara on my phone."

"You and Tara are just friends, right?" Tommy asked him directly.

"Yeah, we're friends. But look at this." PJ said as he showed him a picture of Tara on his iPhone.

The picture was beautiful. At first Tommy thought it was a picture of her daughter, Hope, so he was alarmed. But when he looked closer, he confirmed it was Tara. She looked younger. And she was posing as though it were one of her college pictures. But it was her.

"Is that why your wife wants a divorce?" Tommy asked.

"No, it's because of a lot of stuff." PJ answered. "Did you see Tara's bruises?" He asked further, quickly changing the subject.

"No, I haven't." Tommy replied.

"They're all over her arms." PJ stated as a matter of fact. "Ask her where she got them. She won't tell me."

"Okay, I will." Tommy said.

"If Michael hurt her, I'm going to kill him." PJ said as he walked away to get a cold beer from the cooler and then began to join in with the conversations of others.

That night in her arms, Tara had exposed many truths and secrets of her soul. Tommy found it refreshing the way men and women spoke with one another after making love.

She had spoken of PJ's actions. And she had informed him of his frequent passing by her home. She had also revealed his abhorrent physical behavior, and unstable manner. Though it wasn't in Tommy's nature to disavow her friends, he would not stand idly by, without voicing his concern.

He found PJ's stalking nature, and abusive character traits loathsome, and he told her so, in no uncertain terms. He did not like him. And he was not comfortable with her being alone with him. Though he had tried to be courteous, he didn't believe she had taken it very well.

"We had a meeting of men." Tommy said. "And we voted him out. He's no longer a man, by any means or standards."

As larger numbers of people arrived at the party, they gathered in the grass, around a slowly growing fire pit, in a large half circle, lined with chairs and logs made for sitting. Some were standing and drinking beer. Some were sitting, watching the fire, and drinking beer. While still others, who were younger, joined Hope and Heather, in the opened garage of their parents' guesthouse.

The music played loudly, as the children danced beneath a multitude of colored lights, reflecting upon the disco ball, tied tightly to the ceiling.

And as the fire grew more and more intense, Tara wheeled herself outside and up the slight hill, through the grass, and joined her guests.

Tommy watched her welcome, and converse cheerfully with her friends.

As he met her eyes, he realized that he felt very much the same inside, as the fourteen-year-old boy he had once been. He was hopelessly in love with her, even now. He adored her every move. Her jovial spirit was intoxicating, much greater than his drink.

"My daughter has a crush on you." Tommy overheard Tara say semi-jokingly to Hope's junior high school volley-ball coach, as he stood near them drinking a beer.

Hope's coach was a handsome twenty-something, athletic man.

"We've chosen you to be in our first mother-daughter sexual threesome, a ménage à trois." Tara said as she teasingly laughed.

Tommy shook his head and walked away. Tara had a decisively unique sense of humor.

As Hope stood between her coach and her mom, she blushed and turned away, making an excuse to re-join her friends. Her mom didn't know that she had been pleasuring her coach since tryouts.

Tommy refilled his big red solo cup from the beer keg and took a long cold drink. It had occurred to him, as he watched Tara struggle over the terrain, how she had managed to live so many years in her home, without having pathways created, built for her ease of mobility.

He would later be informed that Michael, who worked for a design firm that created equipment for use of the physically challenged, was intentionally denying her access; not only to their two-car garage but also to his upstairs rooms of their home. A fully functional elevator was in an adjacent room to their kitchen but was pulled away from the wall to disallow it from use.

"Hey." Hope called out to Tommy as she sat inside the lighted garage.

Tommy turned his gaze quickly, finding Hope sitting in a chair wearing short, gray-cotton shorts, and dressed in a

141

small white top. She was long-legged and barefoot, and tauntingly beautiful.

She spread her legs open for him to watch her pull her panties to one side. And then she giggled and hurriedly jumped up and rejoined her friends in their dance.

Tommy swallowed hard.

There are some things in this world that you cannot, un-see. He would never be able to un-see that.

Tommy instantly hated himself.

"God-damn-it." He said aloud as he walked away and sat down in a chair by the fire. He turned back towards the garage door, wondering if that had just happened.

And he caught a glimpse of Hope smiling back.

"Fuck." He screamed in his mind. And then he chugged down a large gulp of cold and foaming beer.

Suddenly.

BOOM. WHOOOOSH. BOOM. BOOM.

The fireworks started.

Multiple bursts of whites and purples, reds, pinks, and blues exploded in gigantic balls of twinkling light. Over and over the sounds of their streaming and the thump of their BOOM brought smiles of joy and delight to the observing crowd.

The lights showed brilliantly in the summer night sky.

BOOM. POP. BOOOOSHHHH. AHHHH.

POP. POP. BOOM. BOOOOSHHHH.

The lights of the fireworks lasted for hours. Everyone had a wonderful time.

And then the rains set quickly in.

Thunder roared, and lightning flashed across the blackened sky as people ran hurriedly to their cars through the rain, with umbrellas and jackets covering their heads.

They said their goodbyes. The party was over. The guests were all gone.

It was two-thirty-seven in the morning, when Tommy and Tara were finally able to talk. Within minutes, they had become deeply engaged in meaningful conversation.

They spoke of their past and they spoke of their futures.

They spoke of their heartaches, and they spoke of their joys. Tommy was so immersed in their discussion that he didn't notice how suddenly it had begun, because somewhere, between the noise and the confusion, the alcohol and the rain, a slowly moving shadow had fallen over Tara's eyes.

Hope had seen the shadow fall. And she knew it was time. She had planned it. She poured a mixed drink, stirring the drug in slowly, and reached it out to him. He would take it. And he would drink. It's what they all had done.

Tommy would remain fully cognizant and aware of his surroundings, though he would not believe his own mind.

He would become deeply captivated by erotic illusion, aroused by the lust of forbidden fruits and pleasures; her forbidden fruits and pleasures; her baby sisters' forbidden fruits and pleasures; and he would not remember their lustful ritual; the ritual of lights.

Heather lit the candles flames, and meticulously spread the ancient Peruvian carpet upon the floor. She laid a red candle at the four corners, North, South, East and West as she had been cultured to do, raising a fifth candle in the air to the center for Above, and placing it down onto the middle for Below. Red is the color of sex, love, power, and vitality. A red candle draws these qualities to you and aids you in any spell work that requires strong, fiery energy.

Hope pushed a button on her CD player and the sound of wind chimes and flutes began to play. She cut the lights and the room went dark, with the flickering radiance and pulsating color of red candles light.

As Tommy lost himself in erotic delirium, they helped him to the floor.

They unbuttoned his long-sleeved shirt, and left it open exposing his chest, and stretched his arms out to full length. Heather unbuckled his belt and pulled it out quickly through the loops of his pants.

While Hope pulled off his boots, Heather unzipped his blue jeans.

"Wait." Hope said. "Not yet. We've got to do it right."

It was one of her rules.

Tommy lay in the shape of a cross, upon an ancient Peruvian rug, painted in the colors of wine and shade.

He lay in the midst of a giant pentagram, which encompassed the whole of the tapestry. As the music played, the children danced around their sacrificial lamb, while their mom stared vacantly into the darkness.

With the flame of the most centered candle, Hope lit the herbs afire, filling the room with scents and aromas of sweet passions and honeysuckle. And then she placed rings of baby-white flowers upon her mothers' and sisters' hair.

As she placed a baby-white ring upon her own, she let loose her clothing.

"To the winds that blow from the four corners of the Earth," Hope said as she sat upon her knees beside her sister, and as they both raised their arms and hands above their heads.

"And unto the waters that bring life, please accept our offerings and our sacrifice this night. We evoke the elements of the earth, water, air and the flame, join us." Heather and Hope finished together.

They prayed to the angels, the goddess of nature, and to the spirits of the air and the water and the trees.

The girls would now perform the Great Rite ritual, the union of bodies that focuses on the masculine and feminine energies in relation to the goddess of nature.

Sex is seen as one of the most powerful energy forces.

And the energy, drawn from the connection between the male and female during the act of intercourse, is used to bring light towards their expected and specific outcome.

And they encircled their sacrifice with salt.

"It is time." Hope said.

Then they looked at him smiling, with ravenous and shameless eyes.

THE DARKNESS IN THE LIGHT

Chapter Twelve – Twelve Rules of Sacrifice 101

There were rules to follow; and they needed to be followed explicitly.

Hope knew this. It was part of her training. The darkness had initiated her education, before she could recognize the differences between the dark and the light. And she had adhered to the principles that had been instilled in her, as well as to the doctrines. There are currently twelve rules in total. They could be taken out of order.

New rules could be added, though none could be taken away.

1. The first rule is Trust. You must gain and cultivate trust in your sacrifice.

2. Infatuation is the second rule. Sacrifice should crave you; desire you, both physically and emotionally. It draws them near; while it is easier if you can exploit their weaknesses, or are so inclined as to be insanely attractive, either way, scenarios can be devised otherwise.

3. The third rule is Separation. A Sacrifice needs to be isolated from their family and friends. You must cut all ties that bind them. Therefore, you become their confidant; the only one they can turn to and depend upon.

4. The fourth rule is Feigned Control. The Sacrifice must feel in control. You must guide them towards decisions that serve your purpose. This vital process works to your advantage when properly executed. A Sacrifice will cast blame upon them, should something go awry.

5. The fifth rule is Endearment. A Sacrifice needs to feel loved and in-love. Create scenarios, allowing loving or affectionate acts to be seen; a memory they can draw upon through darker times.

6. The sixth rule is pleasure. You will own them once you make this happen.

7. The seventh rule is Training. You must instill your expectations in your Sacrifice. They must learn what you desire from them. Training them up in the way they should go is an especially important rule.

8. Marking Territory is the eighth rule. Bite marks, scratches or however you want to do it.

9. Discipline. The ninth rule is discipline. Educate your Sacrifice in the differences between reward and punishment, pain, and pleasure. Be creative.

10. Submission. It is rule number ten. Decide what is the most submissive way to give, or to gain power and control from your Sacrifice.

11. The Ritual of Lights is an all-encompassing rule. It comes in at number eleven because it was added later.

The details must be taught, and the dance must be seen, but this, above all rules, must be done meticulously. With or without sex, it must be done right.

12. The twelfth and final rule is Sacrifice. Sacrifice is the greatest of all rules. They must be willing. Their gift brings enlightenment and the most power and control.

The darkness craves it, and feeds upon their essence.

These were the philosophies and rules Hope had been instilling in Heather. They had been handed down to her, as they had been handed down to her mom.

Hope had not asked about them, because they were secret. And she was good at keeping secrets. But they were more; they were a spiritual guideline, a sacred doctrine. The rules were a necessary process of training Sacrifices to the angels, the goddess of nature, and to the spirits of the air and the water and the trees.

Tommy awakened in a Kroger store parking lot, in Marion Springs, at four-thirteen the following morning, with no memory of how he had gotten there.

He felt scratches on his chest, and he had a pounding headache.

"It must have been one Hell of a party." He thought to himself as he turned the key and started the ignition.

He had no idea.

Then he flipped on its headlights and drove home.

TONY NALLEY

Chapter Thirteen – The Graveyard

He awakened with a jolt.

And he opened his eyes from a solid sleep.

The phone rang at seven-thirty-five. It was late Tuesday evening.

"Are you okay?" An alarmed woman's voice asked. "I've been worried. I've been trying to reach you for hours now."

Tommy shook his head and sat up on the couch holding his phone to his ear.

"Tara?" He asked.

"Of course, it's me silly." She answered. "Where have you been? Are you okay? Are we still on for tonight?"

Tommy's thoughts were still muddled from the party and his head still hurt profusely. As he placed his feet upon the floor and brushed back his hair through his fingers, he tried to seem coherent and speak clearly.

"What day is it?" He asked as he checked the date on his phone. "Yeah, sure, we're still on." He said while clearing his throat. "What time should I pick you up?"

"Well, I wasn't sure if we were still going, so I hadn't started getting ready yet." Tara stated. "Let's see. It's a

155

quarter to eight. So, meet me at the Steak House at nine-thirty?"

"We're on. I'll see you then." He said as she hung up the phone.

He had been in a daze since late Friday night. The last thing he could remember was watching the fireworks show and having a few drinks. He remembered having a fantastic time. And he remembered his meeting Tara's family going extremely well. He also recalled the rain and speaking with her.

They had been speaking heart to heart. He remembered that much. With her girls by her side, she had spoken with him about her childhood pain, and of the hurts she had carried with her throughout her life. But the next he could remember, he was sitting in his car, in the middle of a lighted grocery store parking lot, some twenty-four hours later; wondering how in the HELL he had gotten there.

"I haven't put on a drunk like that in years." He said to himself as he rubbed the back of his head and stroked his beard, "Easily since my twenties."

As he undressed for a shower, he turned the water on and checked his look in the full-length mirror. He wasn't a fashion model or a body builder type, but he thought he looked pretty good for a man of his age. His chest was firm, and his waist was tight, and his arms were nicely defined. He wore size thirty-four jean, the same size he had worn in high school. He was happy about that. Many of his former classmates had ballooned to record proportions since graduation. Tommy hadn't allowed that to happen to him.

He ate as best he could, and he exercised often. He was a single man and he needed to keep himself as youthful, vibrant, and attractive as possible.

"What the hell?" He said out loud as he discovered bite marks.

There were teeth marks firmly imprinted on the left cheek of his ass.

"How in the fuck?" He said out loud as he ran his fingers over his wound.

He hadn't seen them when he'd showered twice before; although he'd admit he hadn't looked closely and had barely been able to hold himself up under the water.

Then he touched the scratch marks on his chest.

"How in the fuck?" He repeated. "What in the fuck did I do?"

He had had some wild and crazy fucking dreams, the last two nights. But that's all they were. Your brain perceives stimuli and stores and processes the information with lightning speed. Dreams are simply the biproduct of the brain's interpretation of thoughts and feelings. Or at least that's how Tommy defined it.

And he'd had some wild and crazy mother-fucking dreams lately.

He arrived a few minutes early for their rendezvous, dressed in black; black jeans, black boots and a neatly pressed black long-sleeved shirt. He was clean and fresh looking with a thinly shortened beard that was neatly trimmed. He wore two rings together, on the thumb of his left hand: a small gold herringbone chain necklace and a diamond earring.

Tara arrived soon thereafter in her BMW. She was an excellent driver. And she had been driving since she was sixteen. She'd honed her skills using long devices that reached the pedals, and she learned to feel the pressures needed for the gas and the break.

Tara was wearing a beautiful blue-bird colored dress. It accentuated her natural southern beauty, and it highlighted her eyes. Tommy handed her a single rose. And he greeted her with a kiss.

"You are beautiful." He said to her, pronouncing each word out slowly.

"Thank you." She replied bashfully. "You're very sweet. Do you like my shoes?" She asked. "They're new. And look," she said as she raised her dress up a little. "You're the first guy I've shaved my legs for in years."

Tara was beautiful. And her legs were baby smooth.

The restaurant was empty at the hour of their arrival. But it was easily accessible and even easier to find a parking place. They had it all to themselves.

Tommy remarked to the young waitress that it made him feel like Elvis Presley, having bought the whole place out.

Tara smiled as the waitress showed them to their table, and as she wheeled her chair up closely across from him.

"Heather just discovered your book." Tara said. "Suffice it to say, she is suitably appalled that we elderly people still think about sex, much less DO it. Dear God, her face." She said as she laughed.

"Please don't let her NOT like me." Tommy replied. "They're a part of you and their liking me is important."

"No, we're good." She confirmed. "She was so proud of the fact that you called her and her friend, 'cool'. That really won her over. I never get over how kids, I don't care how old they are or how much they might act like it doesn't matter, crave your love and approval."

"I've missed out on a lot of your life." Tommy said as he took Tara's hand. "But I am grateful you are now in mine. And I am awfully cute." He said flirtatiously.

159

"You are." Tara said sweetly. "And I am grateful for everything, especially the cuteness."

The food was delicious. Tommy had the steak, butterfly-cut, medium with a twice-baked loaded-potato with sweet corn and peas, while Tara had the roast-chicken with a side-salad, with ranch on the side.

"My neighbor, Millard, was all mad at me." Tara stated with a smile. "He came over the next day and said, 'I've been trying for seven years to get you to spend the night with me and then you spend the night with another man'." She laughed. "I think he was only partly kidding."

"I'll bet he was partially jealous." Tommy replied. "Hell, I'd have been jealous of me."

"He did seem to be. He's such a sweetie." She answered. "If I can live to be his age and still be so engaged and fun, I will consider it a serious blessing."

"Tara, I have to be honest." Tommy said. "Apparently I had been drinking way too heavily, and I don't remember much beyond the firework show."

"Me either." Tara exclaimed and then laughed a little. "I was sitting beside you watching them in the sky, and then nothing. I think we talked a while after the rains came and everyone left, but zilch. We must have had a really great time."

This was the first official date he could remember being on with Tara, and he knew their conversations always ran deep. So, he did most of the listening, and intently paid attention, while devouring his filet minion.

"Another of my deep secrets that nobody knows," Tara began. "My dream has always been to have a chunk of land upon which I could build a few accessible cabins where families with a disabled member could come for vacation and have access to all of the very expensive equipment that will allow them to fish, hike, explore etc."

She continued. "I already have connections to the companies that make that stuff to get things donated. I would love to do this with you. I know how many times I've been told no and how much it deeply hurt, especially after I had kids. I would love to be able to partner with you and give people a week of 'yes, you can'. And not the begrudging 'the law is making me' yes, but 'because I really want you to remember this forever because you deserve it' yes." She continued further. "I don't know how we would get around it but even the national parks build a very limited number of accessible cabins and things that have air-conditioning, which is pretty much a requirement of people with disabilities who have impaired respiratory function. But able-bodied people reserve them years in advance because the park service is doing the renting and they, by law, are not allowed to ask, 'What is your disability?' You have to take people at their word. And people lie all the time. One year, my mom and dad, my siblings and me and the kids, all rented a cabin at a national park in Virginia, and it was amazing.

But word got out and we've never been able to rent it since. The park service is so apologetic because they know that people lie just to be able to rent a larger cabin with air-conditioning at the same really cheap price as the other cabins, but they can't ask questions."

Tommy listened in tentatively as Tara caught her breath and smiled sweetly.

"Sorry, that was so long-winded." She said.

Tara found Tommy extremely handsome as she touched his hand, and then finished her salad. He was genuine and gentlemanly. She hadn't received flowers from anyone in a very long time. And she hadn't shaved her legs for a date since she had gotten married, well before her girls were born. She also found him cute and funny as she reached out with her napkin and wiped sour cream from his beard and mustache.

"What am I going to do with you?" Tara asked him.

"I don't know. But that sounds like one of my lines." Tommy replied.

"Oh, you have a particular set of lines that you use on women?" She asked.

"See there, keep talking like that and I'm going to have to spank you." He replied sheepishly.

"You're a player. I get it." Tara said. "It's all about the game."

"No. This night is all about you." Tommy replied. "Besides, I'm too lazy to be a player. You'd have to come to the sidelines and bring me a cup of coffee." He said as Tara looked at him inquisitively. "I'm not a player …I'm the coach."

He had made her laugh. It was a good thing. He loved to see her laugh. Primarily, he wanted Tara to be happy.

As they finished their meal Tommy left a generous tip on the table and thanked the waitress for being so nice.

"The food and service were excellent." He said as he escorted Tara through the doorway.

"You're welcome." She returned with a smile. "And you smell really nice."

He was caught off guard for a moment as he received her compliment. She was an attractive and much younger girl. But he smiled, and he thanked her anyway.

"It's Obsession." He said with a wink. And then he walked outside to get some fresh air. While he waited for Tara to return from the restroom, he lit up a cigarette and took a long draw.

They took her car. He let her drive. He had a special plan for her tonight. He had been planning it for weeks since the night she fell into his arms. He knew she loved the supernatural, the paranormal and the mere mention of ghosts and spirits. So, he gave her directions to a pioneer graveyard he had researched and had written about in one of his novels.

The way was sullen and dark. Though the pathway that led behind the old and historic jailhouse could be easily traversed, it appeared treacherous and foreboding.

"Should I bring my gun?" Tara asked jokingly though with a hint of seriousness.

"I carry a silver-plated derringer in my pocket." He replied. "I'll take care of you."

The graves of the pioneers were laden with heavy carved stones. The large colonial styles and artistically chiseled markers protected them from the elements. Some were buried beneath the soil and minerals, while still others were buried above the ground, beneath the sarcophagus constructed of stone.

Tara rolled close to a large memorial and sat comfortably with anticipation; while Tommy grabbed the present he had brought for her and placed it upon her lap. The package was decorated with scenes of Martins, a favored bird of her and her father's, and it was laced with ribbons; his gift glowed brightly within its coverings and shone brilliantly through the darkness of the night.

"You could have anyone you wanted." Tommy told her. "I could, too. I've resisted so many over the years, because I didn't feel anything truly for them. With you, it's completely different. Just so you know. I'm a man when I have to be, a boy on the inside. I'm rambling. Sorry. But I'm happy you're in my life, Tara. I truly love you with all of who I am."

"Thank you for telling me that." She replied. "I love who you are, just so YOU know."

"You see the fullness of the moon shining down upon you?" He said to Tara, as he kneeled beside her on the grass. "You are breathtaking beneath its light, but no man has ever reached up and plucked it from the sky and given it to you." He continued as he reached inside her gift bag and revealed her glowing prize. It was round and familiar and glowed in her hands as she received it. "I wanted to offer you the world, but all I have is the moon."

Tara's eyes sparkled, and she giggled unintentionally.

Tommy was an original. And he had placed much thought and depth of meaning in his gift. He was corny, but he had spoken the truth. He was the only man who had truly ever given her the moon.

"This is the most genuine and heartfelt gift anyone has ever given me." Tara said as she took Tommy's hand.

Tommy looked downward into Tara's eyes as she smiled lovingly up at him.

"Carry me to that gravestone." Tara whispered to him as she wrapped her arms firmly around his neck.

He lifted her from her chair and carried her gracefully to the limestone tomb, and she rested herself upon its smooth top, looking up into the moonlit sky.

"I want you." She said to Tommy. "Take me here in this ancient graveyard, upon this pioneer tomb beneath the moon."

And Tommy did.

Beneath the moon; beneath the summer skies; beneath the starlight ever watching.

And she watched him, watching her.

TONY NALLEY

THE DARKNESS IN THE LIGHT

Chapter Fourteen – A Nicholas Sparks Novel

The gentle flowing waters of the creek were cool as the night fell quickly behind the trees. The sounds of the stream echoed softly against the rocks as they splashed calmly upon its banks. It was the ending of a perfect summer's day. It was the beginning of an ideal summer's night.

Tara climbed herself on-board the 4-wheeled all-terrain vehicle with a jovial spirit, as Tommy took the seat behind her and held on to her waist tightly as she revved the engine motor.

"You ready?" She shouted at him above the mufflers roar.

"Let's do this." He replied.

She took the path that led steeply down an embankment beneath the cream-colored concrete bridge. They landed with a splash as their tires met the brook. And the waters splattered, as she drove on through the shallows, and over level creek rock. She drove him to a private place, a secret place where she had taken no other man.

Hope and Heather walked barefoot through the waters behind them, while Ben lagged closely at the rear. He carried the cooler filled with drinks and chips and marshmallows to roast on the fire they would build.

Tommy sensed something here, an elusive presence.

169

Something in these woods was alerted to their arrival.

And as the sun fell quietly behind the tree line, he watched for movements in the shadows.

It was Heather's area of expertise to light the fires. They gathered wood and sticks and fallen limbs, while she fanned the flame that fueled its light.

Hope listened intently as she lay quietly, stretched out upon the ground, while resting her head peacefully on her boyfriend's hairy leg. While Heather and Tommy shared ghost stories and sang songs around the growing fire, Tara's iPhone glowed brightly and vibrated upon her lap.

"It's PJ again." She stated agitated. "I told him I'd be busy, but he just won't leave me alone."

Tommy watched her expression before he turned to see the lights of a vehicle crossing over the bridge. He thought it was PJ's. But he couldn't tell for sure. He mentioned it to her, but she dismissed it fully.

"I'm at the creek with Tommy and my girls." She said to him when she called. His voice could be heard over the speaker, though his words were not clear. His tone, however, was not pleasant.

"Tell him we're seeing one another." Tommy said aloud.

Heather was visibly upset when she heard Tommy's words. But Hope was relieved when she said, "We don't like PJ, Mom. We like Tommy better."

Tommy smiled.

"What do you think about matching tattoos?" Tara asked him as she closed out her call. "Do you like Martins?"

Martins were her favorite birds. They had been her father's as well. Before he had died, he had built her a birdhouse. And they had watched them fly upon the winds together, for countless hours, as they built their nests and trained their babies.

"I'd be willing." Tommy replied.

"Okay then." Tara said with a gleam in her eye. "Did you know that I received a call the other day from PJ, and he asked if the girls would like to help him clean out his garage?" Tara continued as Tommy shook his head, no.

"Hope was excited and said, yes. And she was very enthused until Heather told her I was talking with PJ and not you." Tara laughed.

"Needless to say," she continued. "You could see her smile fade immediately into a frown, and they did not volunteer to help." Tara and the girls all laughed.

"Now, that deserves a hug." Tommy said as he opened his arms to Hope.

171

Ben was not amused when she got up and walked barefoot across the creek rock and hugged Tommy tightly.

Tommy had all but put aside his memory of what Hope had shown him at the party. He didn't remember fully, until she was warmly in his arms.

"I've found a track of land for sale that I think you would like." Tommy said as he let loose of Hope's grasp and quickly sharpened a stick to roast a marshmallow. "It's located about fifteen miles south of here, off highway twenty-one. It's a piece of property, heavily secluded between hills and trees, across a small winding creek. It has two Amish-built log-cabins made of pine, located on the property, with fully updated amenities."

"It sounds wonderful." Tara replied. "You've put some thought into this, haven't you?"

"I like to have a plan." Tommy said. "Yes, and I like to move forward. It's good to talk things through and make hypothetical decisions, but perceptions are more clearly defined when you can use all your faculties. It helps you focus."

"Sounds fantastic," Tara exclaimed. "I'm so excited. I'm just so grateful to have someone who sees what I see and can help me make the push. Once we're in," she continued. "I KNOW I can carry my weight. I just can't do it alone and, therefore, I've never attempted to start it on my own. I wanted to, but I knew I couldn't maintain it alone. And I'm so glad it's you."

"I'm so glad it's me, too." Tommy replied. "I'm so glad you want me to be a part of it all. I don't say anything I don't mean." He continued. "I believe in you. And from my heart and soul, you are loved."

"Thank you so, so much. And so are you." She replied.

"I'm also researching insurance companies." Tommy continued. "We'll need a business license, EIN number and a DBA name for the business."

"I am overwhelmed, impressed, excited and a little scared." Tara related. "But I'm smiling."

While the girls and Ben gathered more driftwood from the sides of the creek, Tommy leaned closely to Tara and whispered softly.

"I've thought about what we've discussed." He whispered. "I don't want Hope and Heather to feel any kind of resentment towards me. They're a part of you, and their feelings are important."

"No, they're fine. There's just no way around it," she answered. "Transitions are hard."

Tommy reached out for Tara's hand, and he kissed it tenderly.

"I am savoring every moment." He continued. "I'm taking my time, no rush, but I'm going to romance you and I'm going to treat you like a princess."

"I wonder what that's like." Tara stated.

"I don't know if you can see it in my eyes or hear it in my voice," Tommy related. "But you make me feel alive, young, and strong. And when we kiss, as I brush your hair back over your ear and bring your lips to mine, you will feel my passion and the truest love you've ever known."

"You are so sweet to me." She said kindly. "It's been a long time."

"I care for you very deeply, I always have. I do my best to be a good man," Tommy said. "But I've got a little bad-boy in me." He said with a laugh.

"Well, that's part of the fun." She answered. "Oh, and I told the girls we spent hours together talking in the graveyard the other night, on our date."

"What did they say?" Tommy asked.

"Heather didn't say, but Hope said, 'Only you, Mom'." She answered.

After the fires had burned down and the brushwood was all gone, they made their way back across the stream.

The eerie feeling Tommy had felt earlier …left him the moment they pulled out of the woods and into Tara's driveway.

Somewhere in the distance a loud howling sound resounded from the woods. It was loud and it reverberated from the tree line. Tara didn't seem to notice. Tommy did. And the eerie feeling came back.

It had gotten late, and Tommy was about to excuse himself for the night, but just then, PJ's truck pulled down the graveled road.

Tommy stood beside Tara in the light before her garage, as PJ parked and exited his truck.

"What are you doing here, PJ?" Tara asked as he walked across the rocks.

"I just wanted to see you and make sure you were alright." He said as he turned to Tommy and reached out his hand.

"You could cut the tension with a knife." Tommy thought as he shook his hand. It was such a cliché, but it was distinctly fitting.

"It's late. I'm fine." Tara responded. "Give me a hug. You need to go."

Tommy would remark to her later that she was confusing him with her actions. If he were only her friend, then she

175

should not pull him closely in her embrace, even when saying goodbye. He watched them hug warmly, and then he nodded to PJ coldly, as he got back into his truck and drove away.

"He's in-love with you, Tara." Tommy said as the taillights glowed red at the end of her road. "You've got a soon-to-be ex-husband living upstairs. And you've got an explosive ex-boyfriend from high school with growing testosterone levels." Tommy said as PJ's tires squalled out, causing dust and smoke to rise above the blacktopped pavement. "And you also have me standing here in your driveway."

"I know. Dear God, we've got a seriously good Nicholas Sparks novel going on here." She said excitedly, "but an actually good one."

Tommy knew little of Spark's writings; though soon thereafter, he found him to be a number one bestselling author. He wholeheartedly believed by her comparison at the time, that he was a romance author, and that he, was playing the role of Tara's love interest; the lead character in a romantic love story; a dream of literature and poetry.

"Want to stay for a while and have a drink?" Tara asked. "The night is still young. It's only eleven-thirty."

"Okay. I'm game." Tommy agreed.

As Tara wheeled herself along the sidewalk to her back porch, and rolled up the ramp, Susie and Bear greeted

Tommy. They licked him excitedly with the slobbering tongues as they made their way onto the porch.

"Bear doesn't usually take up with men very well." Tara explained. "If he's licking you like that it means he really likes you."

"I like him too." Tommy exclaimed as he rubbed Bear and patted him.

"You are very special to me. I hope you know you always have been." Tara stated. "I am so grateful for being able to talk with you about things that have eaten me alive for years. And I'd never spoken of those things. I never would have," she continued. "I don't think. I have never trusted anyone enough to share any of that. We do have a connection that goes way back, many lifetimes. You are a rose of Venus to me and very special. Maybe more to come and I love you, too."

Hope lay upon the sectional couch with Ben stretched out behind her, while Heather sat upright beside them, staring intensely at the fifty-inch television screen as Tara showed Tommy through the doorway to her living room.

Tommy hadn't been inside Tara's home before, though he had spent a great deal of time outside, on her back porch and in her guesthouse.

The room had vaulted ceilings and was decorated with sparsely laden pictures of her children, and two guitars

177

were hung by the entrance ways. The shiny wooden floors appeared smooth to the touch, as her dogs walked upon it noisily with their paws. Upon the tallest wall over her fireplace, was placed a large and animated painting of a castle and a dragon with the glowing moon he had given her, sitting upon her mantle beneath.

"This is our FUCK wall." Heather said as she excitedly jumped over the back of the couch and ran over and pointed it out to Tommy. "We write down things that are funny or stupid, or things that piss us off."

"Yes," Tara confirmed. "That's our FUCK wall."

The back wall of the living room was decorated with multi-colored sticky notes slung haphazardly and in disarray. Tommy read some of the things that were written on the pink, yellow, red, and blue sticky notes, which he now realized were covering the whole of the back wall of the living room.

"Dear Ben," one note read. "I feel really dirty tonight. Please DO me. Love, the Dishes."

"I'm sorry my asshole cat …shit in your bed." Another one read. "Do they make a Hallmark card for that? Love, Heather."

"These are hilarious." Tommy said. "I love it."

"Every time you fart in the living room," still another one read. "A Unicorn dies, Love Mom."

"You like that one?" Tara asked. "They get better. Keep reading."

"I respectfully request your presence in my panties," It was written on a pink sticky note with a large red heart drawn around it. "Love, Hope."

"I really like dicks." Tommy read and then cleared his throat. "Okay." He remarked. Nothing else was written.

"They get better," Hope implied. "You're just getting started."

"I love you for your wit, charm and wonderful personality." Tommy read. "But your cock ...wait, what was I saying?"

"Kiss me softly for a few minutes." Read another one. "Then fuck the shit out of me."

"Wow." Tommy said as he cleared his throat.

"I had the best sex ever." was written on another. "No wait. Oreo's. I had Oreo's."

"You call it a dirty mind," was written on a red sticky note. "I call it a sexy imagination."

"I want sex that is so nasty," upon a blue message was written. "There'll be no question that I'm going to hell."

179

"That one was mine." Hope said. "I have a few of them on there."

"Read one of mine." Heather said excitedly. "Here, read this one."

"Do you like pizza?" It read. "Cuz I wanna pizza dat ass."

"These are really interesting." Tommy stated, though he was obviously becoming concerned.

"Sorry your dick is all wet," another one read. "I licked it, so it's mine."

Tommy looked around and he caught the smiles and sparkling stares of Tara's girls. Tara was smiling at him, too.

"Some of them are little risqué and raunchy." Tara said. "But it's our way, and nobody needs to worry about it, you know?"

"Yeah," Hope interjected. "And whoever says anything about it gets their name added to the wall." She said as she laughed.

Tommy turned back to the sticky notes that were scattered randomly upon the wall.

"When someone asks me a stupid question …" another note read. "It is my legal obligation to give them a sarcastic remark."

"Spread me wide and lick my sweetness." On a pink note, was written. "Taste my creamy white upon your tongue. Signed: The Oreo Cookies."

"When someone tells me I look familiar." One note read. "I tell them I do porn."

"I've got my period," another one read. "You're free to go."

Tommy turned away from the wall.

THE DARKNESS IN THE LIGHT

Chapter Fifteen – Fraternal Order of Police

His blood boiled as it coursed through his veins. His fires ran hot, sending waves of adrenaline into his heart that pounded deep within his chest.

"Fuck her!" He shouted aloud, as he beat his steering wheel with his palm. "I don't fucking need this shit."

His big white truck squalled tires all along the road in front of her house as he pushed the pedal to the floor.

She'd been toying with his emotions for months. And because of her texts and pictures, he was losing his house and half of his bank account, to his wife of twenty-five years, who had recently filed for divorce.

He knew Tara was still married. They had talked about divorcing their spouses.

"But damn it to hell. It wasn't supposed to turn out like this." He thought. "And now, there is another guy in her life?"

He had seen them by the creek. That's why he had texted her. He wanted to know if she would lie to him. When she called, he had been sitting in her driveway.

"What the Fuck?" He said to hear the words out loud. "Fuck her."

PJ was a good guy. Tara had told him so.

183

He started mowing grass and cultivating lawns right after graduation. And he and his brother had started a business that had become very successful. He made good money, and he lived a comfortable life. It was hard work, but it kept his body fit and trim, and he preferred physical work over sitting behind a desk any day.

He had cheated on his wife a few times. But it wasn't his fault. His wife had grown fat and had become a real bitch. He brought the money home while she sat on her fat ass and ate Hostess Twinkies. And she handed out sex like she was rewarding him. He wasn't her child, and he wasn't a fucking dog either. But she held the reigns to his 401K and bank accounts. That's why he had stayed so long. He'd wanted out for a long time. Tara had come back into his life and provided him with a solid reason to break away. He'd loved her since they dated in high school.

He didn't know how to deal with this.

She had kissed him, and they had fucked. Though he would admit that it was only one time, and she had been acting very strangely the entire night. But that's when she had also let him take pictures of her with the camera on his phone. They were great pictures. He masturbated to them every night. They were the same ones he had gotten in trouble with.

Tara was wild in bed. She was incredible. Her body was unbelievable. He did, however, have to do most of the work, because of her loss of use of her legs. But she was

184

willing to do anything. She drove him absolutely fucking crazy.

He liked the feel of being in control, too. She made him feel strong. He was already muscular, but she made him feel like Superman.

He pulled into the diner just outside Marion Springs at eleven-fifty-five.

There were three police cars sitting in the parking lot.

Two were sitting side-by-side with their parking lights on. They were talking with one another with their windows rolled down. He could see their silhouettes clearly through the reflections on the windshield glass.

The other car was empty. The officer was sitting on a bar stool inside. So, he walked inside, and pulled up a bar stool beside him.

"Hey Kenny," PJ said as he slapped his friend on the back. "Time for a doughnut break, huh?"

"Hey dumb-ass," The officer replied. "I'm having a beer. What brings you out tonight, Hot-rod?"

"I've got a problem." PJ answered.

"What's her name?" Kenny replied with a chuckle.

"You met her a few weeks back." He replied. "Same one."

"She was the pretty girl in the wheelchair? I do remember. Tara wasn't it?" He said as he drank from his beer can. "So, what's up? Did her old man find out?"

"Nope, another guy's come into the picture." PJ answered as he ordered a drink for himself.

"Fuck man. That's not good." Kenny replied. "What are you going to do?"

"I don't know." PJ said as he took a sip of liquor and sat the glass down hard upon the bar. "Got any suggestions?"

"Don't do anything stupid that will get you arrested." Kenny said. "But you need to push back. Scare him off." He continued as he finished the last of his beer. "Put a knife in his tire; or something that can't be traced back to you, but something that will get your point across."

"Damn brother." PJ said excitedly. "I'm getting advice on committing a crime by a member of the police department. That calls for another round."

PJ was a member of the Fraternal Order of Police. He liked the prestige and the credibility that came along with being a member. He donated funds and he brought them industrial sized coolers, filled with ice and cold drinks.

And, when he had installed the blue flashing lights on the top of his truck, he didn't feel as though he would be ticketed for turning them on, because of his membership.

PJ turned his flashing blue lights on often.

He had even pulled some vehicles over, though; he didn't pretend to be a police officer. He just found it funny, after he had pulled them over, when they found out that he was not a cop.

He had even made Tara laugh doing it.

He wanted to join the police force when he was younger, because he liked the feeling of being superior. People respected the badge, and women loved a man in uniform.

But he would not pass the test because he couldn't read too good.

"I've got to get back on the road." Kenny said as he declined his offer. "I'm on duty until five-thirty in the morning. You should go home and get some rest. But thanks for the offer. I'll take a raincheck."

PJ had another shot of whiskey and a coke.

There were a lot of things running through his mind.

He also had a problem getting close to Tara's girls. They avoided him. And he did not understand why. He had helped them fix their ATV's when they had broken down, and he had even brought his friend's heavy equipment over for them to drive.

Heather didn't talk to him at all.

While Hope would talk with him, she was still very stand-offish.

PJ drove his truck past Tara's house again, for the last time tonight.

It was one-thirty in the morning.

Tommy's car was still there.

He hated that bastard.

TONY NALLEY

Chapter Sixteen – By Another Guy's Name

"What do you think about Twilight?" Heather asked Tommy as he sat down upon the soft leather cushion beside her, and Tara handed him a drink.

"I have to be honest, Heather." Tommy answered as he sipped from his glass. "I'm not a fan of sparkling Vampires."

"That's awesome." Tara shouted. "See girls, I told you he was one of us."

"Okay." Heather continued. "What do you think of Harry Potter?"

Tommy could tell he was going to be on thin ice if he didn't answer this one correctly. But he wasn't going to lie.

"At first, when the movie became popular, I didn't think I was going to like it." He answered. "But, I have come to like Harry Potter very much."

"Yay." Hope shouted as she prayerfully clapped and sat up on the couch. "Now, Heather," Hope continued. "Ask him the most important question."

"Is Professor Snape a good guy or a bad guy?" Heather asked intently as she widened her eyes and smiled at her mom and sister.

Heather absolutely loved Harry Potter.

She had read all of J.K. Rowling's books and she had seen every one of the movies. She also had a collection of memorabilia that would rival any true Harry Potter fan. It included a real magic wand from the franchise. It was made exactly like the wand owned by Seraphina Picquery, former President of the Magical Congress of the United States of America.

The wand was crafted by Violetta Beauvais …and was, like all Beauvais wands, made of swamp mayhaw wood with the "hair of the Rougarou" at its core.

Like Seraphina Picquery's wand Heather's was also thirteen and a half inches long. It had a purple jeweled handle, unlike the pink jeweled handle from the props, and was ebony, tipped with a silver clasp around it.

In the story, the wand selected its owner after the 'Sorting Ceremony' and attracted a lot of controversy as Beauvais wands were known to be quite comfortable with performing Dark magic.

"I've thought about that myself." Tommy replied. "My son and I've talked about it extensively."

The girls and Tara were on the edge of their seats, as they waited with anticipation for Tommy's answer.

"Professor Snape had been in-love with Harry's mother since they were children. And he had lost her affections to a boy who teased and ridiculed him for years at Hogwarts." Tommy lamented. "While he loathed Harry because of his father, he protected him because of his love for Harry's mother. When he killed Dumbledore, he did it because of a promise he had made to him. Dumbledore knew he was dying and had planned his death as a way for Professor Snape to become seated closely with Lord Voldemort."

Tommy sat back upon the couch, took a drink, and he watched their eyes.

"Long story short," He said. "Professor Snape was a good guy."

"NOOOOOOO," Heather and Hope both shouted.

"YES. SWEET," Tara shouted with delight. "The house is EQUALLY divided."

The girls discussed their opposing opinions briefly with slaps and stomping feet while Tara gloated in their bickering. Tommy took the opportunity and began massaging Tara's back. She hurt the most below her right shoulder blade. He continued to massage her thoroughly as he asked the girls and Ben and Tara, a trivia question of his own.

"Okay, my turn." He said. "In all of the Walt Disney animated movies, if tried by a jury in a court of law; who was the absolute worst evil villain?"

"Cruella De' Ville." Heather shouted.

"Nope," Tommy replied.

"But she tried to murder puppies for their fur to make coats." Heather said emphatically.

"She wasn't that bad." Hope answered her. "She didn't kill any of them. I think it was the Evil Queen in Snow White."

"She did try to kill Snow White." Tara said inquisitively looking at Tommy.

"She would be convicted of attempted murder, if she hadn't been killed." He replied with a wink. "But she's still not the worst."

"The wicked fairy, the Witch in Sleeping Beauty," Heather shouted happily.

"She would be found guilty of attempted murder before her own death as well." Tommy said smiling. "But no."

"It was Jafar in Aladdin." Hope shouted. "He pushed that guy into the tiger's mouth in the desert and tried to kill Aladdin and everybody."

"Close," Tommy answered. "But no one would have convicted him because the man he pushed was also a criminal. And not only would he not have been missed or have had a missing person's report filed, but there was also no evidence that could prove Jafar guilty of having pushed him in. The only witness was his talking Parrot."

"Iago," Hope shouted excitedly.

Tommy nodded his head, yes.

"Exactly," Tara exclaimed.

"Frollo," Ben interjected. "He's the worst villain."

"Wrong set of movies, Genius," Hope answered and corrected him with a slap on his leg. "He's the guy in The Lord of the Rings, stupid. And they're not Walt Disney cartoon movies."

"No, not Frodo," Ben replied defensively. "Frollo, he's that old dude in the Hunchback of Notre Dame, who had locked Quasimodo in the Bell Tower, and who had also tried to burn Esmeralda at the stake."

"Ooh, yes, he was a bad guy." Tara stated. "Good answer, Ben."

"I forgot all about him." Heather said. "I agree. Good answer Ben."

"I'm sorry." Tommy stated as Hope hit Ben hard on his leg with a thud.

"He's still not the one." Tommy continued. "I think there would be charges filed for arson, kidnapping and

195

imprisonment, as well as for attempted murder. While he is a very evil villain, and it was an excellent answer, it is incorrect, no, he's not the worst."

"Okay, I give. Who was the absolute worst evil villain in all of the Walt Disney animated movies?" Heather asked begrudgingly.

"Does everybody give?" Tommy asked as they all shook their heads, yes.

"It is Scar from The Lion King." Tommy answered. "He murdered his brother and he also drove Simba to run away, by causing him to believe the death of his father was his fault. He then sent the hyenas to kill and eat him, so he could ascend the throne as King." Tommy explained as they sighed and saw his points were valid. "He was guilty of murder, attempted murder, and treason to the royal crown; as well as the near devastation of the kingdom."

"That was a really good piece of movie trivia, Henry." Tara said accidentally to Tommy. "That feels so good." She said in response to his message.

Tara had called him by another man's name.

Heather and Hope gasped.

"I'm sorry. I meant, Tommy." Tara recovered. "Henry was my friend, and you remind me a lot of him. We were

196

very close. In many ways, we were as close as you and I." She explained while looking into Tommy's eyes.

"You were, friends?" Tommy said with emphasis on the vowel.

"Yes, we were friends." She answered. "He threw himself off a bridge in Pennsylvania." She continued. "I was with him only hours before. He gave me no warning signs. He was a good friend. He committed suicide."

"That's awful." Tommy replied. "I'm sorry for the loss of your friend, and for his family's loss. Why did he kill himself?"

"He was a good man." Tara stated as she reached out for Tommy's hand. "He didn't leave a note. But I like to think he died for love."

"I'm so very sorry." Tommy replied sincerely as he stopped his massage and kissed Tara sweetly on her back. He looked around the walls to find a clock. "What time is it?"

Heather jumped up as the dogs began clawing at the door to be let out, and she walked outside with them as Tommy and Tara discussed the time.

"It's almost one-thirty-five in the morning." Tara answered.

"I've got to be going then." He replied. "It's getting late."

197

"We have to run Ben home anyway." She said while laughingly looking over at Ben. "His parents like to see him once in a while, too."

Tara's iPhone dinged and buzzed upon her lap.

"And there is this issue, which I apparently have to deal with right now." She aggravatingly related. "By the way, I think I just got dumped by PJ, and I'm trying to figure out why that really hurts my feelings."

"Hmmm," Tommy hummed, "Because you have a kind and caring heart?"

"I don't know. It was a bad situation. Even though I know that it's just that is the only kind of relationship I've ever stayed in. It's that overbearing 'prove to me you love me' crap. I don't know why. And I know I don't want that. And I know people don't change. But maybe I can't change either. Maybe I need to just go away and die alone. As pathetic as that sounds, it keeps everybody safe."

"You are a wonderful caring and loving person." Tommy said. "Your heart wants to love everyone. Your mind and spirit know better. You are worth so much more than an overbearing, intimidating man."

"Tommy, you are so sweet." Tara related. "I'm so sorry that we got reacquainted and then it just turned into some insane Shakespearean nightmare. I'm truly sorry."

Tommy was relieved. At least he wouldn't have to deal with that situation any longer. PJ was a jerk anyway. He thought he was an ass. And he wasn't completely sure why Tara had remained so close to him.

"It doesn't matter because it's over now." He thought to himself, as he breathed a deep sigh and called the issue closed.

Tommy said his goodbyes to Ben and the girls, and he walked outside to his car. Bear and Susie met and escorted him, as was their custom while he petted them lovingly and playfully, and opened his car door and got in.

He'd had a great time. He had enjoyed Tara's and her family's company very much. But he noticed his car wheel turning sporadically as he headed down the graveled driveway. So, he pulled over in the grass and found that he'd gotten a flat tire.

"Damn it." He exclaimed in the dark of the night.

The lights of Tara's car blinded him as she pulled up alongside him in the dark.

"Flat tire?" She asked.

"Yes." He answered.

"Get in." She said to him. "We'll take Ben home and come back and figure something out."

"He can sleep in my bed, Mom." Heather said happily as Tommy sat down in the front seat.

Heather's room was filled with broomsticks and magical wands from the Harry Potter collection. But she didn't like sleeping in her room alone. She preferred sleeping on the pull-out bed in the living room with her mom.

"It's settled then." Tara stated. "It's late and you're sleeping over."

Tommy did stay over, but he couldn't sleep.

His mind was still filled with questions. So, he sat outside and felt the coolness of the summer morning's breeze, through his un-buttoned shirt, as Tara poured them both a cup of hot coffee, and they spoke for a while.

There were things he needed to know. There were questions he needed to ask. There was a promise he had made that had tormented his soul.

They spoke of Dan, and Tommy listened, as Tara revealed her pain.

"He's a pastor at a large Baptist Church in Georgia now." She said. "I've wanted to let him know I've survived, and I haven't forgotten. You know?" She continued. "When our old church burned down in Miller's Creek, did you know that he was the last person in the building that night? Did you know that? He was also the last person inside another church, where he was a Minister and it burned down as well, ironic huh? It was exactly under the same circumstances. And yet another church burned in two-thousand-fifteen. His church ministry is called Church two-thirteen. He has a history of arson."

Tara paused.

"And did you know?" She asked. "Dan called my mom on the phone and told her after I had broken it off, that I had been instigating the whole thing and that I had 'come on' to him …and that I had seduced him. Did you know that? And my mom believed him." Tara said as she began to weep. "And then my mom …my mom …called a family meeting at the dinner table and told my dad that I was a whore and a slut. Dan had given her intimate details. She said everything out loud and told my dad right in front of me. She told my dad I was a whore. I was fifteen. And to this day …my mom believes I'm a slut. And my dad …he died believing everything my mom had told him."

Tara wept openly as Tommy tried to console her.

"I've always wondered if he's hurt anyone else, you know?" She asked the question. "And if he's hurt any other children. It keeps me up at night. I have nightmares. I wonder if he has been molesting and raping children all along."

Tara's facial expressions changed while she began to formulate her next words.

"I remember terrible things." She said. "I remember horrible things."

And then she looked at Tommy and said, "You're the only good I still remember."

"Do you remember the night of your accident?" Tommy asked her. "Do you remember the rock concert and the ride home?"

Tara had no memory of going to a concert.

But Tommy remembered vividly.

Chapter Seventeen – The Rock Concert

"This band is so fucking awesome!" Tara shouted to
Tommy through the pulsating lights and the roar of the
crowd, as the beat of the drums rocked the stadium.

From side to side, she waved both hands high above her
head, and danced to the thump and the rhythm of the
music; letting all her youthful inhibitions run wild.

It was a school night, but she didn't care. She skipped
school when she wanted, and she stayed out as late as she
wanted. Nobody controlled her. Nobody would. Not even
Dan. He didn't know where she was tonight, and she
didn't give a damn. She didn't belong to him. She wasn't
his property.

Dan's physical abuse had grown progressively worse
with each passing day over the last two years they had
dated, and she had come to loathe him. So, she kept
herself inaccessible to him as best she could. And she
removed herself entirely from his schedule. She knew he
had been watching her. But she couldn't deal with his
bullshit any longer. She wanted to be free of him.

Tara was dressed in her tight little blue-jean shorts that
showed off the curves of her hips very nicely. Her
matching white strapless top left her midriff uncovered,
allowing everyone to see her slim, soft abdomen and her
cute and newly pierced bellybutton. She wore her knee-
high suede boots to amplify both her sensual and sexual

THE DARKNESS IN THE LIGHT

side while completely rocking her black lace choker necklace to augment her submissiveness.

Tara was complete and total jailbait.

She was fifteen years old, and she owned it.

Everything had changed over the past year of Tara's life.

She had become the definitive party girl. She was a sophomore in high school, and she was a dancer for the drill team. She went to Band Camp over the past summer and learned to twirl and spin flags with the marching band. She also loved to run and play basketball, so she joined the track team and played on the girls' junior varsity basketball team. But she had to say goodbye to her church because she no longer believed in God. She quit the morning after Dan had driven her home. It was also the morning she had lost her baby, but she never told anybody that, not even his father. She had buried him without a marker beneath her Angel tree.

Her grades had unexpectedly improved over the last few months. Perhaps due to her feigned interest in her older male teachers, or in their noticeable interests in her. But as her grade point average grew, so did her tarnished reputation. She drew jealous looks and hateful glares from older women and girls her age. But she didn't care.

Getting guys to take her places and buy her things with the expectation that she would give them some, gave her a thrill.

The boys wanted her. Men wanted her. And she loved it.

She loved the attention.

Her confidence in her abilities to manipulate the male-ego escalated with each new encounter. It stimulated her self-assurance, although it also caused her darkness to become more dominant, and more prevalent. It caused her sense of shame and remorse to disappear, completely.

Her brain was becoming compartmentalized, allowing a new personality to emerge. Her thought processes were separating different incompatible cognitions from each other. The darkness fell over her quickly. She couldn't control it. Even more frightening, she wasn't aware of it happening.

She had blackouts. She had awoken alone once, hundreds of miles away from home, with no memory of how she had gotten there, beside a man she didn't recognize.

Large and increasingly larger amounts of time were gone, vanished from her memory. And as her blackouts became more prevalent, the detachment of her feelings grew.

The guys who had brought Tara to the rock concert fawned over her like she was a piece of candy. And she loved it. It was the first time she had been out in a long while. It had been at least two weeks. And she hadn't seen Tommy socially, since Band Camp. That was two months ago. He had grown taller and more muscular since the last time she had been this close to him. He seemed more masculine and confident in his faded blue jeans and more sure of himself. And he smelled good too.

Tara played her part well. She flaunted herself openly and she teased Tommy with her flirtatious touches, dancing close to him, pressing the softness of her backside up against his groin. All the while she wiggled her hips, daunting his masculinity with her feminine charms.

She knew what boys liked. She knew what boys wanted.

And she played modest and demure to his advances while stroking his male ego at the same time.

She danced for hours as they listened to the band's music playing loudly together, through the stadium speakers.

And then, once the last band had finished their encore and the Concert was over, she and the boys all piled back into the car they had arrived in and headed for home.

She crawled into the backseat with Tommy. From the front seats, she heard a beer can tab pop open, and soon they were passing around a twelve pack between them: with foam spewing out over the sides and dripping all over the car's interior.

Tara got lost as the alcohol induced her mind. She pulled her boots off, exposing her pretty legs to Tommy, as she placed her feet in his lap. She poured down another one, chugged back yet another, and laughed as some of it came out her nose making her spew and spill it all down the front of her white top.

"Wet t-shirt contest, Boys," Tara yelled out. "Who's got the prettiest pair of titties?" She shouted as she crawled up through the car's sunroof, raised her arms up over her head and waived them in the wind.

"Babydoll pretty." She shouted into the night air, flashing her wet t-shirt and boobs and perky nipples to passersby who were driving down the highway.

The guys in the car couldn't see her face or hear what she was saying through the roaring sounds of the music blasting, and the air that came rushing in through the opened windows. But they could see her wiggling in her tight shorts, with the top half of her rocking the rest of her body through the opened roof.

The darkness fell over Tara's mind as the alcohol lowered her resolve and inhibitions. She wasn't herself as she climbed down from the sunroof and sat on Tommy's lap.

Within the inner most recesses of Tara's mind, her personalities now struggled for power and control. She had always allowed the dominance of the darkness to take her at will. But her love for Tommy caused great emotional conflict within her.

Her mind was flooded with thoughts of his pain and disapproval. She knew he wouldn't understand. She knew he still loved her. But her life had taken such a turn for the worse. And she had fallen so far down the rabbit hole, that she was afraid to even kiss him.

She couldn't tell him what she had gone through; what she was going through. He had seen the changes. And he had heard the whispers and the lies. She wished she knew how to love him.

Her love was a poison that she did not want him to drink.

And then her world went dim.

Her lights went out.

A shadow fell over her eyes.

And the darkness took control.

Between the lights and the shadows from the road, Tara nestled herself tightly against him, coveting his warmth, nuzzling his neck with brazen kisses, and she rested herself in his arms.

And she was consumed by the darkness.

"Where am I?" Tara mumbled in slurred speech, as her blurred vision revealed two shadowy outlines in the front seat of a car she couldn't remember getting in to.

"Why can't I remember? Where have I been? What have I done?" She asked herself as she looked around.

"You've been asleep for over an hour now." A calming voice spoke to her. It was Tommy's voice. He had been holding her in his arms. "You asked to be dropped off here. But we can take you home if you'd like."

He had been holding her the entire way home from the concert after she had fallen asleep in his arms. He had checked her breathing. He had felt her heartbeat. And he had kept her warm by covering her in his jacket while she slept.

Tommy brushed the hair from Tara's eyes over one ear.

"Are you okay?" He asked. "I'll take care of you."

They were sitting in a Kroger's store parking lot, alongside a car that one of Tara's friends owned. It was a long red car from the seventies; it was a gas guzzler, a nineteen-seventy Ford Thunderbird; a metal tank on wheels.

Tara stared at the car through the window, as she reflected upon Tommy's words.

"He said that I had asked them to drop me off here. And that my friend would drive me home once she got off work." She recalled in her thoughts. "I don't remember any of that. But it sounds plausible."

"I'll be alright." She whispered. "I had a wonderful time." She said, this time her words were slurred as she stretched and yawned.

211

And then she kissed him.

She kissed him warmly, revealing a beer flavored aroma on her breath.

"I think I was going to fuck you tonight." She whispered playfully in Tommy's ear before she got out of the car barefoot and holding her boots.

Tommy didn't understand. They had just been together, but she was acting like she didn't remember. He smiled at her inquisitively, as he thought of her kiss.

"Now try to sleep with that vision in your head, my honey." Tara said.

Tommy watched her stagger slowly to her friends' car; open its door and climb in, and land with a thud.

"Thanks for going with us, Tara," one of his friends in the front seat yelled out the window.

"Are you sure you don't want us to drive you home?" Tommy asked.

"I'll be fine." Tara mumbled. "My friend will be off work soon."

She didn't know that for sure. She didn't know what time it was. She barely knew where she was. She couldn't remember anything since getting home that afternoon from school. She didn't remember asking her friend for a ride either. She had only just recognized her car.

Tara didn't remember going to the Rick Springfield concert or the names of the cover bands that had performed. And she didn't remember being with Tommy.

She remembered being dropped off in the Kroger store parking lot, and she remembered being left there alone.

But what Tara remembered vividly, however, was what had happened ...only moments after Tommy and his friends had left her there alone.

to be continued.

An Author's Request

"I deeply appreciate the time you gave to read this story. And I would be ...incredibly grateful ...if you were to share your thoughts with me on Amazon. The story does not end with Tara's memories that she's shared with Tommy ...there is more ...there's a great deal more and I am continuing this saga."

"Please help me get more reviews. Tell your friends about this Novel and add your comments. The best reviews could be included in the next addition to this series."

Tony

THE DARKNESS IN THE LIGHT

Made in the USA
Columbia, SC
16 November 2022

70994418R00131